ROBERT GILBERG

Starvation Mountain

Contents

Prologue

April 25th, 2013

"It was an all-white space, sort of like a fog drifting around me. You know, like the place people who've almost died, or did die for a minute, talk about? He was standing there in the middle of a gravel road, leaning on a motorcycle parked sideways across the road, gesturing at me and mouthing something I couldn't hear. But I watched his mouth moving and figured it out: he was saying, 'Stop, go back. Go back to her . . . .'"

One – Annie

December 2012, A small avocado grove on Starvation Mountain, San Diego County, USA

The striking view from the property boundary, uninterrupted for fifty miles looking north, focused on the long east-west ridge of snow-covered Palomar Mountain. A deep blue Southern California winter sky, filled with fluffy white clouds and a stiff, chilly breeze left behind by the now past winter storm revived him from last night's excesses. Mt. San Gorgonio—another long, much higher, snow-covered mountain—one hundred miles as the crow flies from Jim's avocado grove on Starvation Mountain, was visible far north of Palomar. You had to know there would be a mountain there; most people, not into geography and landscapes, would simply pass it off as another low-lying cloud on the distant horizon. But Jim Schmidt knew it was a mountain. He'd been up there and loved it. He loved it all—the entire Southern California landscape that had become his motorcycle playground after he moved to San Diego from Boulder Creek in the Santa Cruz Mountains of northern California. Standing at various high points in San Diego County, Jim could point to and identify each peak visible in a full 360-degree sweep. He'd hiked or motorcycled to most of the summits.

Jim remembered Annie and his disappointment when she said she wasn't ready to move to Southern California with him when he first moved there. But she'd given him a little hope when she added that a few months after he established himself in San Diego she'd come down for a week to decide if she wanted to make the move, too. It was two years before she finally made the trip, but it wasn't what he'd dreamed. He knew there was another man in the picture.

On the drive to the airport the last day, Annie said, "I don't think it'll work out, Jim. There's the other guy I'm with, and I've been upfront about him with you. I thought coming down to spend time with you would help me sort things out. To some extent, it has. What I mean is . . . I still care for you, but something from our days in Boulder Creek is missing. I don't feel it anymore. It's probably me, not you, Jim. My new job . . . Jeff . . . time moving on . . . it's just not the same."

Those were the words he didn't want to hear: "It's just not the same . . . ." She was right though; it wasn't there anymore. Beginning the week, he believed it still was—for him—but it didn't seem to be for her. Their conversations seemed forced too frequently, minutes passing before something more was said, with him having to push the dialog along. Their love-making had been perfunctory and with little passion, even though he'd given it his all. He could sense she was just going through the motions. It was clear the old love had ended, and with the passing days a discomfort slipped between them. It finally was over; they both could see it in the other's eyes—before they looked away—afraid they'd have to talk about it. They both knew, but hadn't admitted it yet.

He knew what she would say before she said it on the way to the airport. CS&N's song was running through his mind, *Just a song before I go, to whom it may concern . . . .* Still, he irrationally hoped that by some miracle he'd be wrong and she'd tell him she wanted to think more about it.

"Let's stay in touch, Jim. We've been good for each other. Who knows, maybe things will change, and it'll be our time again. But right now, my life is in the Bay Area and I want to find out where things are going with my job."

"And with Jeff?"

"Yes . . . and with Jeff."

What . . . and I keep hanging on by a thread with an occasional phone call?

But Jim had held onto that thread for years. His adult life was passing by while he held onto that thread with an occasional phone call and a rare "Hi, how are you, good to see you" lunch when he was in the Bay Area, but both avoiding prolonged eye contact.

In some crazy way, the mountain-side avocado grove—he liked to call it a ranch—would be the answer. Annie had loved living up in the Santa Cruz mountains with Jim, and he figured—hoped—this grove, with its spectacular building site would give her the motivation to reconsider and bail out of the Silicon Valley rat-race to find peace in the Southern California mountains with him.

She was interested, she said, during that last call, a few years later. She'd drifted away from Jeff, and the job she held for the past several years had turned sour. A promise to come down again for a week in the following month never happened. A multi-truck, multi-car crash on the Bayshore Freeway, the hideous 101, had killed her. She'd been on her way to a mid-day appointment with a promising new client looking for new marketing concepts.

The avocado ranch-home idea had become bittersweet for Jim. Being up there on his now more frequent visits, sitting alone on a cut-off tree stump, made him love her memory more as he imagined what life there could have been with Annie. It also brought on heartsickness that, over time, he forced himself to shake off—but only partly—finally deciding the best thing he could do—the only thing—would be to somehow move forward. But the loneliness was always there: *I need someone . . . .*

These were the most beautiful of San Diego County days, with the air brisk and clear; the hillside vegetation, now with months of accumulated dust and grit washed away, deep green and healthy looking after the long, dry autumn of Santa Ana winds and burning heat. The last storm had been the third in a series of north Pacific storms hitting the county since October. Instincts told Jim the backcountry wildlife would once again be saved, with trickling streams, brimming water holes, and vegetation swelling with new moisture. How the wildlife made it from the last rains in March, or sometimes April, until October at the earliest amazed him. San Diego's backcountry was an arid high desert, demanding that only the toughest plants and animals survive. Now that cooler winter temperatures prevailed all around the county, with the backcountry freshened by the rains, he was ready to get on one of his motorcycles and cruise.

It was late December, the magical southern California time during the break between Christmas and New Year's holidays, when the entire county quieted down as people took a break from the buzz saw of everyday life. An unusual serenity seemed to have descended on the county for a few days. There was snow on the mountains, and it was a balmy seventy degrees at the beaches.

A guilty feeling came over him. *I haven't been up here since harvest last September; I've owned this place for five years now, but I'm finally going to do something with it*, he promised himself. It had five hundred avocado trees on five acres and a spectacular building site on the northern property boundary overlooking the San Pasqual Valley, fifteen-hundred feet below. A perfect place for the modern house he'd always visualized, with a deck looking out over this fabulous view, and room underneath for a garage full of motorcycles.

This spring, after the trip . . . .

Two - Penny Lane

February 2013

"When will you complete the final drawings?" Jim asked the architect as they walked back toward the Suburban parked off Starvation Mountain Road. "I want to get them out for bids and select my builder by May, or June at the latest."

"I'll have them ready by the end of this month or early March, depending on how long it takes to get them signed off by County Development Services. They'll be ready for bidding."

"Great! Call me if you have any issues with how the driveway splits around and under to the bike garage." They stopped by the Suburban's driver's side door.

With a wave and "No problem," the architect pulled the Suburban away from Jim Schmidt, leaving him standing by his motorcycle parked in the tiny gravel pull-off that served as the only usable parking spot on the entire length of the property. *I've got that out of the way, now I can get back to planning my trip* . . . . Jim turned to take one final walk back to the building site.

"Hey mister, nice bike!"

The voice came from a lanky California blonde in form-fitting jeans, flip-flops and a T-shirt that looked a little too cool for the brisk weather. It was a sunny southern California winter day, but Jim needed an insulated vest over his flannel shirt for motorcycle riding. He guessed her to be in her mid-forties.

She walked toward him from a small cabin at the end of a gravel driveway surrounded by the avocado trees of the adjacent grove. Jim had noticed the cabin when he first bought his grove, but never had seen signs of occupants until now: no lights in the windows, no cars in the driveway, no chairs, barbecues, or tables outside—nothing to suggest anyone lived there. He'd decided it must be used only when whoever owned the grove made occasional visits to check up on the crop's health, or at harvest time. The owner's visits had just never coincided with his. Of late, he'd ignored the place, but was surprised to see a late-model Mustang convertible parked in the driveway that morning when he arrived with the architect.

"Hi! Thanks, it's my favorite."

"Favorite. Like, are there more bikes and this is the best one?"

"Yeah, there are a few more. Who are you?"

"Penny. And who are you?"

"Jim, Jim Schmidt. I live down in the La Jolla area. Penny who?"

"Penny Lane."

"Sure, you are. I guess that's a line you give everyone when you first meet?"

"Well, that's not my birth name. But when your last name is Lane, how can you avoid it? My real first name is Emma, but some kids in school started calling me Penny when they discovered old Beatles music. Everyone liked it, so that's who I've been since the '80s."

"I like it, Ms. Penny Lane. Emma is a little too old fashioned for me. I had an aunt named Emma back in Indiana a long time ago, but no Emmas in all of my school days in the '70s. Up till now that is. You know Penny Lane was a street in Liverpool, and not John Lennon's girlfriend's name, don't you?"

"Thank you, Mr. Jim Schmidt," Penny said. "Yes, I know that. Most people do think Penny Lane was one of his school-days girlfriends; but I don't care, it's a cool name. So, what's going on? I saw you walking around with rolls of drawings and that man. Are you going to build something?"

"I'm building my getaway home. I'll be taking an early retirement soon and want to move away from all the traffic and hassles of living down there in the fog and too many people. So, I bought this place a few years ago for that reason."

"You're not going to cut down the trees! You aren't, are you?"

"God, no. The trees are what brought me up here. I'm going to leave all of them except a few that will have to come out for the driveway back to the building site at the north edge of the lot."

"Can I see what you're going to build?"

"Sure, let's walk back there and we can look at the drawings when we're standing right on the building site."

Penny Lane walked close by Jim's side, smiling and watching him, elbows occasionally bumping, as they stumbled across the uneven grove land.

"Sorry, didn't mean to lurch into you like that," he said.

"That's okay, it's a little hard walking in here." Somehow, she liked the feeling. *He feels safe.*

He thought she could be a good friend and looked forward to telling her about his dream house.

The sun was dropping toward the low mountains to the west when Jim said, "Penny, I have to stop going on about myself like this before I bore you to tears. I've been talking for hours now and need to leave. I hate riding some of these roads after dark."

"Jim, I love what you are going to build! I hope you'll invite me over after it's done."

Thinking he wanted to see more of her, Jim answered, "Sure. Love to. But since you're here at the cabin, we can get together occasionally and have a glass of wine as it goes up. Do you like wine?"

"It's okay. Jack Daniels is better though."

"Penny, you don't know what that means to me."

"What, that I like Jack Daniels?"

"Yes . . . yes, that you like Jack Daniels. I always offer wine because that's all anyone seems to drink in California. It's the socially acceptable thing, I guess, so that's what I offer. I drink a little wine when I have to, but I'd rather be sippin' Jack."

"You and I will be soul mates. Neighbors and soul mates. How do you like that?"

"I'm beginning to like you, Ms. Penny Lane, even though I don't know anything about you. The next time I'm here, we'll talk about you."

"Okay, but we do know some important things: you like motorcycles and I like motorcycles, you like Jack Daniels and I like Jack Daniels, you like living up here in the trees and I like living up here in the trees. That's a pretty good start, Mr. Jim Schmidt."

"Yeah? You like motorcycles, Penny?"

"Sure, want to see mine?"

"*You* have a motorcycle?"

"Yes. It's right behind the cabin. It's a Harley Sportster."

"Show me."

Penny walked Jim around to the back of the little cabin in the neighboring grove where the Harley was sitting on its kickstand under a generous, corrugated sheet metal lean-to roof, enclosed by the back wall of the cabin and vine-covered trellises hiding more corrugated sheet metal sides.

"I'll be dammed! An Iron 883 Sportster with the black on black finish. How'd you come by this beaut'?"

"A friend."

"A friend?" Not knowing whether to ask more, Jim hesitated, leaving the question hanging there.

"Yes. My friend Mack. I'll tell you about him sometime; maybe when we have that glass of Jack Daniels."

"But, it's yours? Or is it a loan or something?"

"Sort of a loan. I don't have the paperwork for it, but I can use it like it's my own. I rode it for the first time yesterday to get used to it. And I'll use it to ride around North County for the next few days."

"So . . . is . . . is the cabin yours? Are you going to be my full-time neighbor? I haven't ever seen anyone around here in the five years I've been coming up here."

"Not really mine . . . it's sort of a loan, too. Same deal. I don't have paperwork for it, but I get to use it as my own. That's if I keep it up and watch the grove."

"Your friend, Mack?"

"Yes, Mack. He's a pretty good guy. A little strange, but pretty good."

"So, when I called you Ms. Penny Lane, was I right in doing that? Or should it have been Mrs. or Miss?" Jim asked, being careful to use the accepted pronunciations.

"Ms. was about right."

"Okay . . . I think," Jim replied. *Hell, I still don't know . . . but I'm not going to press it.*

"How often do you ride motorcycles?"

"On and off; whenever I get a chance, which hasn't been very often lately. But I'll be riding it every day while I'm up here."

"Maybe we can hook up for a ride together. Maybe up to Palomar Mountain and around Warner Springs? That's one of my favorite rides."

"I'd love it! Or over to Idyllwild on Mount San Jacinto? That's one of my favorite rides. We could do that too."

"It's a little longer, but I like that one, too. And there are some good places for lunch up there. It'll be your choice! How long are you going to be up here?"

"No definite plans. I'm sort of footloose and fancy free these days. A week, a month, a year; depends . . . ."

"Sounds like a good plan to me. I like your style, Penny Lane. Give me your phone number and I'll call when I'm going for my next ride."

"Well . . . how about this; I'll give you my email address and you can contact me that way."

"There's no internet connection up here, you know."

She pulled a cell phone from her hip pocket and waved it at him, saying, "I can get my email with this."

"Okay, sometimes I go on the spur of the moment, but we can try that."

"Actually, Jim, I'd prefer it if you give me your email address and phone number and I'll contact you, one way or the other."

Strange how she's backing off after the way she approached me. "Whatever you want. I like you and think we should get to know each other more. After all, we're going to be neighbors. Look, I've gotta get back down to yuppieville," the name he gave to the wall-to-wall hamlets packed along San Diego County's coastal strip. "Here's my business card. My email and phone number are on it."

He smiled as he fired up the smooth-running BMW 1200, saying, "Glad we met, Penny, looking forward to hearing from you when you're ready to go. I'm planning on riding next weekend, if you want to go along then."

"I'll let you know. Nice meeting you, too."

She reminds me of Annie and our time up in the Santa Cruz Mountains. Jim walked the BMW around in a tight half circle, waved at Penny, and nudged the throttle. The Beatles' tune, *I've just seen a face, a face I can't forget . . .* reverberated through his mind as he twisted the throttle, hard. His tail light disappeared in the twilight and avocado trees surrounding the road.

Three - Mack

*N*ice guy, Penny thought to herself as she listened to Jim's motorcycle rev through its gears after turning onto Highland Valley Road, which wound around and below the avocado groves, heading west, downhill toward Lake Hodges.

She took her time, ambling her way back to the cabin, thinking over the few things Jim had told her about himself, and the differences between his life and hers as she compared him to the men she'd known and associated with. Jim had a Ph.D. in computer science and worked in satellite communications at a small, secretive firm over in Sorrento Valley. That followed his years up in the Silicon Valley area, working on highly-confidential military communications systems in a place in Mountain View, which he laughingly had called, "the Blue Cube". *Or something like that. Whatever—it all sounded mysterious.* He had friendly eyes and a warm, safe-feeling voice.

Ex-husband Bruce was now in her distant past . . . *and Mack's in jail!*

Penny had been counting on the arrangement Mack had offered her the previous month after she'd quit her job in tears and disgust. The commercial property management work she'd been in for over ten years had devolved into life in a pressure cooker, with Penny the piece of meat slowly being turned into something unidentifiable and ugly. She had to get out. George, the business owner and her boss, was squeezing everyone: the tenants, the maintenance workers, contractors—and her—to pay for his gambling habit at the local Indian casinos. He was losing his ass and trying to make up for it by increasing the rents, decreasing the upkeep, and refusing salary increases. She was making the same salary since her last raise three years ago. And she was caught between unhappy tenants screaming about needed repairs and the last rent increase, and George screaming at Penny for paying too much for needed painting, or plumbing repairs, or unrented office space. And then there was the recent touching . . . . Too frequently, after a new bout of friction between them, George tried to compensate by placing his hand on her forearm—which was okay—but when it became a touch on the shoulder, she'd wanted to brush the hand away, but in the interest of harmony, ignored it. Then it was no longer the near shoulder; he started reaching across her back to her far shoulder. Nearly an embrace. Too much. Way too much! What next?

Fuck it! Fuck George! Fuck this job! She'd called it in one Friday morning without a plan for what she'd do after the call. *Who cares? I've had it with this bastard!*

She ran into an old high school classmate and occasional college date, Mack, that night in a café-bar in downtown La Mesa.

"Hey, Penny, how are you? You're looking great!"

It was what she needed to hear that night. And after an evening spent talking about life since high school, exes, and bad jobs, ending the evening at Mack's snazzy apartment in Mission Valley, Penny thought she'd made the right decision to leave her job. But she wasn't sure about the decision to spend the night with Mack. He was a fun guy in their college days, but had always left her feeling a little sleazy. She'd considered that but convinced herself, for one evening, she didn't give a damn. And maybe he'd changed over the years: who knew? But he hadn't changed and a faintly sleazy feeling was still there. She decided to blame it on the joint they'd smoked; after all, she was forty-eight and could damn well do as she pleased. She was a little disappointed in herself, but it wasn't going to bother her. *It's just one night!*

The next morning, drinking coffee with Mack on the apartment's balcony overlooking the pool and three spas confirmed both: she felt a little sleazy, but also a little better about things:

"I can offer you a job."

"Really? What is it?"

"I need someone to look after my books and keep track of the assets in my businesses."

"I can probably do that. I have a degree in business administration from State, you know. What are the assets? Are we talking about properties, or equipment, or financials . . . what?"

"I know you have that training; that's why I asked you. Let's just say it's financial. Not much in the way of physical stuff, but there is some of that, too."

"I need a little more. Are we talking about stocks and bonds, some kind of investments?"

"Loans. I make hard money loans. I need help keeping track of them."

Disappointment in her voice, Penny answered, "Oh, I don't know anything about that. I've never even known anyone in that business."

"Now you do. It's pretty simple and I can teach you everything you need to know. Right now, I'm sort of keeping it all in my head and in a little notebook I carry around. But I need someone to clean it all up, track stuff, and computerize it. Are you good with computers?"

"God, yes! When I wasn't on the phone taking crap from someone, I was keeping track of everything on spreadsheets, sending out notices and emails. I can probably do it."

"I know you can do it. And there is some actual property stuff that needs to be managed, too."

"Like what?"

"Bike stuff. I buy and sell motorcycles and motorcycle parts. I've got a warehouse up in Ramona where I keep it all. There's a nice office inside where you can work. I'll set it up with the newest PCs, internet, phones, furniture, microwave . . . everything you'd want."

"Ramona! I live in San Diego. I'm not sure I want to make that drive every day. Highway 67? Suicide alley!"

"The money's good."

The money was good. After hearing the salary offer, Penny decided she could manage the sleaze issue by being tough and keeping everything on the professional level—and Mack at arm's length. She accepted the job and started the following Monday, working from home while Mack was getting the office set up. She Googled everything she could find on hard money lending. And she started compiling, from random sheets of paper and Mack's—not one, but three—notebooks, information about the loans he and a previously unmentioned partner had been making.

Three weeks later Mack showed her the office he'd built for her in the Ramona warehouse, located across the road from the Ramona Municipal Airport. It was all he'd promised, with cable internet, multiple PCs, multi-function printers, office furniture for two, and a kitchenette with a conference table. And there was an old, oak, roll-top desk and a large, heavy safe. The office was located nearest the road, with the warehouse space in the back part of the building, all surrounded by a gravel parking lot. But the property left much to be desired. The building was a run down, corrugated metal affair—shack might have been a better word—that had seen its best days, and was far enough from the downtown area to discourage quick runs to convenience stores for lunch or snack foods. Without the sounds from the airplanes warming their engines on the nearby taxiways, or in takeoff, it would have felt very isolated. She shuddered at the thought of needing to work late hours after dark; the place was just too lonely. But the money was good . . . .

Penny moved in—and a week and a half later, Mack disappeared. In the month she'd been working with Mack, Penny had grown used to not seeing or hearing from him every day. Not even every two or three days. This time it was a week. He finally called—from the downtown San Diego County jail. He wouldn't say why he was in jail other than that it was some big misunderstanding that his lawyer would handle. But, in the meantime, he couldn't come up with the ridiculous bail they'd set at two hundred thousand dollars. The judge told him he was viewed as a flight risk because of the seriousness of the charges and his frequent travel to Mexico. Mack didn't mention the details of the charges.

"Watch the warehouse. Don't let anybody in. I mean nobody. Tell me that you understand and agree."

"Okay, Mack. Whatever you say."

"Good. Look, if you're tired of the drive up there, I have a cabin close to Ramona on Starvation Mountain in an avocado grove I own. My dad left it to me when he died, and he wanted me to look after it. You can use the cabin if you want to be closer to the warehouse. It's old, but clean and kind of a fun place. It has satellite TV, a fireplace, and a nice view of the valley. You might like it. And the drive from there to the warehouse is a piece of cake, you don't have to mess with Highway 67."

"Oh? Why do you think I'd want to live there? My place in San Diego is fine."

"I don't want the drive to become a problem for you, and I need you working for me now, with this going on."

"Mack, I don't want to get caught up in something."

"You won't. You just started and none of what I'm going through will splash on you."

"But what about this partner of yours in the money lending business? Can't he do this?"

"No, he's not much for numbers and stuff."

"But money lending is all about numbers and stuff, Mack."

"I know, but I never depended on him for that. He's more like my debt collector; you know, reminding people about their payments when they get a little bit late . . . ."

"Does that mean he's your 'muscle' when you need it, Mack?"

"No, not so much . . . . He's got money of his own in this and, let's say . . . has a special interest in getting paid back. Gary, my partner, can be very persuasive since he knows the law. He used to be a paralegal, so he's very valuable to me."

"Mack, if this goes on a while, how am I going to get paid?"

"Gary will get your checks to you. And he'll bring you the receipts for loan payments, deposits, and stuff. He'll get in touch. Look, he's a little gruff and rough around the edges, but don't be put off by him. He's a good guy."

Gruff? Rough around the edges? Can't wait to meet him . . . .

"Mack, you're making my old job look good. I'm getting nervous over this."

"Calm down. Don't go getting all female on me. Look, I need you to help me. I'll come up with a nice bonus for you when I get through this."

"All female? What the hell does that mean?" Deciding she wasn't going to be put down by Mack's chauvinism, Penny said, "Look, I'll give it a couple of weeks, Mack. But you've got to get this cleared up by then. I don't need any bullshit."

"Ok, fair enough. I'm going to count on you. If you do use the cabin, there's a Tom Henry—he lives on up the road a few mailboxes—who manages the grove for me. If you see anything that looks like it needs attention, go see him. He's a good guy and will take care of it. You can tell him to drop the expenses off at the cabin and we'll work out how you can pay him."

"Sounds like you'll be out of action for a while, Mack."

"Nahhh, I'll get this settled before you know it. Just planning for all contingencies. That's what makes me a good businessman."

"Look, I'll go up there and check it out. But, I'm not making any promises about the cabin, or, for that matter, anything longer than a couple of weeks."

"Great. I think you'll like it. It's yours for as long as you want it. The cabin key is in a cubbyhole of that old roll-top desk I moved into your office. And there's a key for a new Harley that's in a little storage room behind the cabin, too, if you want to do some riding. The bike's key is in there, too. Look, I gotta hang up, the guards are starting to watch me."

"Bye, Mack."

"I'll call you Monday. Sorry about that 'all female' crack."

"I don't think you are, Mack. Bye." She hung up.

The next day, Saturday, Penny went to the cabin to check it out. It was a rustic, cute little place that she decided wasn't too bad and did have the advantage of being much closer to Mack's Ramona warehouse. And the new Harley Sportster was irresistible. She rode the slick machine up to Julian as a test ride, marveling at its power and handling as it effortlessly climbed the uphill grades and glided through the downhill curves. The downhill runs made her remember her skiing days on the slopes of Mammoth Mountain and Lake Tahoe: the days when her marriage to Bruce was still new and their love felt strong.

She ran across a group of motorcyclists, including a few old friends from her married days, on Julian's main drag and accepted their invitation to cruise the Sunrise Highway with them. They stopped at the restaurant near the Mount Laguna Lodge for refreshments. Warm remembrances from her time of riding all over Southern California with Bruce and these friends flooded her mind as they sat at a long table, everyone huddled around Penny, asking about how she was and what she was doing these days. On her return ride back to the Starvation Mountain cabin, she second-guessed her decision to jump from a bad job to possibly a worse job with a man who might be a criminal as her new boss. *My God, what am I about to do; holing up in a cabin on a remote mountain like a hermit and working in a shack out at the Ramona Airport? I want to be with old friends again. This is crazy, I'm spending tomorrow calling everyone I know looking for leads to a real job.*

"Oh . . . hi, Mack. How's jail?"

"Shitty. Thanks for asking. Did you go to see the cabin?"

"Yes. It's not too bad. I like being up on the mountain."

"Are you going to use it?"

"I think I will, for a little while anyway. I told you I'd give this a couple of weeks to see what's happening with you, so I might as well give myself a mini-vacation on a pretty mountain."

"Did you find the keys to the bike?"

"Yes, and I took it out for a spin up to Julian. I love it; nice bike."

"Were the keys where I told you?"

"Yes, in that old desk. I wondered why it was there along with all the new stuff you brought in."

"It was my dad's. Sentimental, I guess."

"Do I need to be able to open that safe?"

"No, you won't need to get into it. I'm the only one who knows the combination and I want to keep it that way."

"Fine. By the way, the Harley does make the deal a little more interesting—and I like the idea of spending some time up there with nature."

"Good, I knew you and your husband were riders, which is why I mentioned the bike. Look, a couple more things: Make sure the steel bars that lock the big roll-up warehouse door are in place. One on each side. Don't leave it locked with just the padlocks. And make sure you use the double deadbolt locks on the office door when you leave. I want that place locked up tight. Keep the shutters closed, too. And there's a tool room off to the side of the bike parts area that is to be locked all the time. I have some valuable, hard-to-replace tools from my dad in there."

"Okay, Mack."

Mack wasn't finished. "Nobody but me has the key for it—well the cops actually have it right now, along with my other stuff—so don't worry about it. And, by the way, there's a phone up in the cabin that's turned on. You can't call me here unless it's prearranged, but I can contact you up there with it. The number is printed on a little sticker on the handset."

"Sounds mysterious, Mack. Do I need to be worrying about something?"

"No, sweetie. I'm just very cautious and want to keep my good things safe. Don't worry. By the way, do you have a cell phone?"

"Sweetie" sent a wave of revulsion through her stomach, and she knew she didn't want to have him calling her away from the office. "Yes, but I don't want to give the number out. I only carry it in the car for emergencies," she lied. "The best way to get me is at the office in Ramona or up at that cabin."

"Want your privacy, I guess. I can understand that. Okay, take good care of things until I get this settled."

That was the last Penny had heard from Mack by the time, on Saturday, three days later, Jim showed up at the grove next door. She now had a very uneasy feeling about Mack and his businesses. Worrying her life was becoming adrift, she was glad to have met a guy she believed to be a stable, mature man. But she was uncertain about everything now. She'd always been able to manage her life—even after losing her husband—and had held a responsible position for years until bailing on it that day. But now there was a nervous feeling in the pit of her stomach. She knew that she needed to keep Mack and his deal at arm's length—and be ready to get out if things got any stranger. *My God, I need someone—a rock to hold onto.*

Four - Old Friend

"Steve, I'm outa there at the end of March. I'm hanging it up."

"What are you talking about? You're not quitting, are you?" Jim's longtime friend and work associate, Steve Barton, asked. They pulled the little strips from their fortune cookies.

"Retiring. I need to just breathe for a while. I shouldn't have gone back; my consulting gigs were just fine. I want to walk away from the bullshit and hassles that go with this corporate world. Ha, it says, 'You will find yourself at the intersection of life and dreams.'"

"What? How can that all be on that little strip? What does that mean?"

"Whatever I want it to. That's what they all mean. Ambiguity has its advantages."

"How old are you? Are your finances set?"

"Yep. Been planning on an early retirement for the last year or two. They let me add the last couple of years I've worked there to the first twelve, so I get a pretty decent retirement benefit. I'll be fifty-eight next September 30 and I'm going to take the company's fifty-five-and-out-early plan. I always said I wanted to be able to quit in my fifties, so now's the time."

Steve placed his beer glass down on the little napkin, "September 30th? Do you know about that date?"

"Sure do. James Dean died when he crashed his Porsche up in the Central Valley, September 30th, 1955; my birthday. Actually, he died, and I was born minutes apart—between 5 p.m. and 6 p.m. Another beer?"

"No kidding! Two Hoosiers, one going and the other coming at the same time? No thanks, I have to drive back to Julian in a couple of hours, so I'll just finish this one."

"I need another, too much garlic in this Kung Pao Chicken without more beer," as he signaled the waitress for another Ching Tao. "Do you think the food quality has slipped since we've been coming here? I need too much beer to wash it down, lately. Anyway, the story is that a guy turned left in front of him on some lonely farm-country road, and it was a left-front to left-front, head-on. Dean was on his way to a race he planned on driving in the next day."

"I didn't know any of that. I was thinking more about Truman Capote being born then," Steve said. "Not 1955, but 1924."

"Why were you thinking about Capote?"

Steve glanced at his fortune cookie strip and balled it up into a little wad before dropping it into his beer bottle. "Nothing important, I just watched a replay of 'In Cold Blood' the other night on TBS and they had some information about his life at the end of the movie."

As he leaned away, allowing room for the waitress to deliver his new beer, Jim asked, "Not a happy way to spend an evening. Did you watch it with Ali?"

"No, she said, 'No way am I watching that again . . . ever!'" Steve said, feigning masking his eyes with both hands.

"I don't blame her. I'd rather watch 'Rebel Without a Cause' for the tenth time than that."

"You a big Dean fan?"

"It's funny. I'd never heard anything about him until I was fourteen years old, when I started watching old movies that used to play after the eleven o'clock news, you know? I watched that movie one of those nights and got hooked on how he looked and with his acting. So nonchalant and cool, but burning up inside with all kinds of tension and passion. I wanted to be cool like that. So I started wearing a ducktail haircut, an unlit cigarette hanging out of my mouth, and everything—at fourteen! But that style didn't make it later on in the sixties and seventies. People were all gone on the Beatles and Stones by then. But I was still hooked on oldies before they were oldies: Little Richard, Elvis, Chuck Berry, those guys. I guess I've always been a little out of step."

"So, what are you going to do when you retire? Play golf?"

Jim slid his chair away from the table to allow enough room for him to cross his long legs, "Jesus, I hope not! Work on my motorcycles, drive them around the country . . . you know, whatever I feel like doing when I get up that morning."

"Got a bucket list?"

"Fuck that! I'm not thinking about stuff like that! I figure that's when I'm going to be born again—not dying. And I don't mean that in the religious sense; I mean it's when I become whoever I've always supposed to have been."

"Yeah . . . I can understand that. But, don't you have a few things you've always wanted to do when you can just say, 'screw it, I'm gonna do this or that?'"

"Yeah, I have a couple of those. One is to drive my Porsche up to Cholame where Dean died that day and, even though I don't smoke anymore, light up and smoke a cigarette, stand there, hands in my hip pockets, slouching a little, and think of him and Natalie Wood. If I have a shirt with a collar on, maybe I'll turn it up a little in the back. If it's a cold day, I'll wear a black leather jacket. Or maybe I'll ride one of my motorcycles up there. He loved riding cycles."

"Are you going to do it on your birthday, September 30th?"

With a frown, "No, too many people will be up there on that day. I'll do it soon after I retire."

"What else?"

Jim leaned forward, and enthusiastically said, "A long motorcycle trip. I'm thinking about retracing the 'Easy Rider' route from L.A. to New Orleans, but without the Death Valley part. Too damn hot on a motorcycle for that, and I never understood why that leg was included, anyway."

A surprised, envious look came over Steve's face as he said, "That would be cool. Loved that movie. Nicolson, Hopper, Fonda, Karen Black . . . ."

"Yeah, and the music. In '69, when that movie first played, I was fourteen and looking for something I wasn't sure I understood. And I was still looking when I left Indiana to join the Marines out here in '73."

"Sounds like being a fourteen-year-old teenager in '69 was a big year for you: first seeing 'Rebel Without a Cause' on late-night TV, and then 'Easy Rider'?"

"Yeah. The world changed for me the day I saw 'Easy Rider.'"

"Ha, me too. I left Ohio for a new job out here just after that movie came out. I didn't like my job back there and had been looking for something better. Better was California and microcircuit design—and the lifestyle. So tell me, what was it about that movie that made you feel that way? The motorcycles?"

A wistful look came over Jim's face as he folded his arms across this chest. "Maybe. It certainly wasn't the story line or dialogue—which was all kind of juvenile. It was the music—the folk-rock coming out of L.A. and San Fran back then. I'd been hearing some of it on the radio before that—but wasn't into it. I guess it was the whole thing; the music combined with the bikes and the scenes when they were riding through the west . . . . The coolness of it all melded together in a way that I've never been able to forget. Peter Fonda replaced Brando for me—right then. I wanted to feel like I thought those guys felt—seemed to feel, anyway—and live where there are mountains and deserts and oceans. And I wanted to be where that music was being created. Indiana didn't have anything like that: nothing but country and western—and cornfields that went on forever."

"Yeah—same thing for me—the sixties and going to California. Fabulous times."

Jim frowned, "But—you know they all hated each other after they made that film—trying to claim who wrote it, who produced it, who directed it; blah, blah, blah. Too bad—I lost some respect for them after I read about that. Hollywood greed, I guess."

"Tough—they all got rich off it! Well look, Jim—old friend; its one-thirty and I've got a conference call with a client. When are you going to tell the company?"

"Soon as I get back." As he stood to leave, Jim asked, "Hey, what did your fortune cookie say?"

Steve looked perplexed, trying to remember, then said, "'Your turn to help old friends will be soon.' What the hell do you think that means?"

"Same thing, whatever you want it to. Give Ali a hug for me."

"Will do."

Jim did as he promised Steve that same day. He worked out a four-week departure with a fat going-away bonus for his innovative work on a new satellite data coding system—and the early retirement package. He never gave it a second thought.

At home that evening he decided to celebrate with a bike ride somewhere the next day—Saturday. Destination yet to be decided.

I wonder if that Penny gal would like to go along . . . .

Five - Idyllwild

When she heard the Harley growling up Highland Valley Road—a few hundred feet below the cabin, and then turning onto Starvation Mountain Road—Penny walked out onto the weathered, broken boards of the little stoop that served as the cabin's front porch. Pulling her sleeping shirt tightly around her legs with one hand she watched as Jim slid onto the gravel driveway leading to the cabin.

"Hey—Penny—thought I'd drive up and see you. I'm going out riding today and wonder if you want to come along."

"Hi Jim—so you ride Harleys too? Didn't think BMW riders would stoop to ride American iron."

"Actually, they're my first love. I rode little 125cc Harleys before I was fifteen back on Indiana farm roads. But I have others too: the BMW, a Honda, Suzuki, an old Triumph, and a BSA. So, do you want to come along?"

"God, yes. I need some fresh air. You *are* the right man at the right time." Penny said, emphasizing the *are*.

"I don't know what I did to deserve that, but I like it. Ride with me, or do you want to ride yours?"

"I'll ride mine . . . I mean, you know, the one that's on loan to me."

"Okay, let's go to Idyllwild."

"I'll put some jeans on and be ready in a flash."

Jim admired her legs, exposed well above her knees, as she twirled around, releasing her grip on the tee shirt to open the screen door. He imagined her wearing nothing under the tee shirt. Van Morrison filled his head: *Do you remember when we used to sing, sha la la la la la, brown- eyed girl . . . .*

She did know how to ride a big, powerful bike. Penny handled it effortlessly through traffic on the I-15 freeway to Temecula where they turned off, east-bound on the two-lane road traversing high desert country to the little community of homes clustered around a convenience store-gas station called Aguanga. After Aguanga, the road became a fun and scenic route through the higher desert country leading to the mountains of the Cleveland National Forest, southwest of Palm Springs.

A fast rest stop for a bottle of water at a little restaurant near the Pacific Coast Trail, full of hikers getting hot food and a fast hot-water wash-up, and they were on the final leg of their trip, through the sparse pine forest and past Lake Hemet at the southern foot of Mount San Jacinto. It had been an easy ride to the little mountain community of Idyllwild, with Jim marveling at Penny's skill at motorcycle riding. He'd made a point of riding behind her to see how she handled the Harley; watching her hand motions on the throttle and brake to see how early she noticed potential road hazards like wet or sandy surfaces, blind intersections, or dangerous traffic conditions, and how she reacted to them all. Her reactions told him she had years of riding experience.

Sitting in an outdoor patio at a little Bavarian-style restaurant overlooking the downtown Idyllwild area, Jim asked Penny how she became a skilled cycle rider.

"Had to if I didn't want to spend weekends alone. I married a guy after college who was a weekend Harley rider. You know, the closet biker types who are bankers, lawyers, and business owners who like to feel a little wild on weekends? Bruce was one of those types."

"I'm guessing you didn't want to ride on the back all the time, and so you learned to ride your own bike."

"Riding on the back is okay for short distances, but it makes me too nervous."

"Because you're not in control?"

"Yeah, scares the shit out of me, actually. You see cars coming in from the side and wonder if he sees it too. Or you see a wet spot up ahead and wonder if he's going to miss it . . . . Lots of stuff that made me want to have my own hands on the bars and controls . . . even though he was a good rider."

"Was?" Jim immediately regretted asking the question. Eyes closed in apology, "Sorry . . . I don't want to be intrusive."

"It's okay, it's been a long time. Was—until the big accident. It nearly killed me, and he was killed," Penny said, emphasizing *was*.

"Jesus! What happened?"

"Jerk started a left turn in front of us. Bruce was riding just off the centerline and didn't have time to move to the right. I was on my Harley, behind and to Bruce's right, which gave me a little time to move over. The car driver claimed he didn't see us coming, and that we were going too fast for him to stop in time to avoid us. It's the standard bullshit excuse."

"Yes, I know. Seems like that's the cause of most motorcycle accidents."

"And that's another thing that had me riding my own bike. I want to be right in the middle of my lane so I have time to react to shit happening on either my left or right."

"How bad were you hurt?"

Penny closed her eyes, taking a minute to breathe, "Very bad. I glanced off the idiot's left fender and hit a tree: broken arms, broken leg, fractured pelvis, bruised kidney . . . . About the only thing that wasn't broken was my head. But, Bruce always bought the best helmets; so, you know, if you're lucky your head's okay; it's just the rest of you that's all fucked up. He went through the car's windshield and died in the backseat of the jerk's car with a broken neck."

"I'm sorry Penny. I didn't know my questions would take us there. I'm surprised you still ride."

"That took a long while."

His interest increasing, Jim asked, "What made you go back?"

"The freedom. I was just holing up at home or working all the time. I wasn't having any fun. You know how it is, when a marriage ends, most friendships end too? I felt like I was dead."

Jim nodded and said, "Makes you wonder about those friends . . . ." He listened as Penny went on.

"One night I was sitting up, sipping a Jack on the rocks and watching movies, when a replay of 'Easy Rider' came on the Turner movie channel. I watched it and realized I needed to find that feeling of freedom again. My repaired Harley was still sitting out in the garage, so I went in there and just sat on it that same night. Must have sat on it for half an hour, imagining the wind in my face, the power under my seat, that leaning into the curves feeling again, and the pull of the road. I was out riding it the next day."

Jim smiled, "'Easy Rider!' Jesus, I have a story about that movie, too."

"Ha, I think everybody does. It was one of those movies that captured a whole generation. I think we're two peas from the same pod, James."

"Yeah, avocado trees, Jack Daniels, motorcycles, what else . . . ?"

"We'll have to find out," she said with a friendly, pretty smile and teasing eyes.

"Ha! Maybe those two peas should get back together—in that same pod? So okay, Penny, I've just decided to tell you something. I don't want to be too pushy, and forgive me if this sounds it, but . . . ." Jim hesitated, not sure if he should mention it.

"But, what?"

"I'm taking early retirement in four weeks and I've been thinking about doing something soon after that for a long time now."

"What is it? Tell me."

"I'm thinking about retracing the 'Easy Rider' route, following old route 66 from L.A. to New Orleans on my Harley."

Penny's eyes opened wide, "Oh, my God! I'd love to do that. Are you going to ask me to come along?"

"Well, I was thinking you might be interested. And I can see you're a good enough rider to do it, but it's at least four days each way. Is your butt seat-hardened enough for that?"

"I don't know, it's been a long time since I've ridden all day."

"And this will be day, after day, after day. You wouldn't want to get two or three days out and find yourself with seat sores or a backache and have to give up."

"I know. Then I'd have to ride back, alone . . . ."

"Okay, so here's an idea; I'm thinking about a long one-day trip, or maybe two shorter days, next weekend. If you want to go along, you can see how it feels."

Intrigue showing in her eyes, "Hmmmm, that might be a good idea. Where are you going?"

"Up in the Central Valley to a place called Cholame. It's around three hundred miles. Do you want another coffee?"

"No, I'll just get a bottle of water for the trip back. Central Valley? Nothing but farms and flat roads. Doesn't sound like a fun ride . . . why are you going there?"

"Okay, don't laugh, now. I've been wanting to go up to the place where James Dean got killed in a car crash for years. There's a little memorial there where people passing by stop to pay their respects. Some even make a special trip each year to be there on the day he died in 1955."

"Oh, I've heard about that. Like people go to Paris to see Jim Morrison's grave! Why do you have such a fascination with Dean? He was a long time ago."

"Long time ago . . . yes, I hate to think of it that way. I was born on the same day he died in 1955. Sometimes I think a little of him passed through me as I was coming into the world and he was going out. Sort of like ships passing in the dark, blinking their spotlights at each other, I guess. I've always wanted to go up there and see if I feel anything . . . I don't know . . . mystical or something, I guess."

"I'm sorry, I didn't mean to imply that you're old. I can understand what you're after with this. Do you believe in reincarnation? Is this a reincarnation thing?"

"I didn't take it that you meant I'm old, hon. But it does remind me that time is passing. No, I don't believe in reincarnation. But I'd like to think I have a little James Dean in me."

"You do? Why, what would you like that to be?"

"Independent. Making it on my own. Living on the edge . . . . Doesn't everyone want that: not living a boring, routine life?"

Penny looked surprised and said, "Independent I can see. Edgy . . . I'm not sure about that. You don't seem like the edgy type to me."

"You didn't know me in my Bay Area days . . . ."

With rolling eyes, "Yes, and I don't think I'll ask about that, either. But I don't see you as a person from that '50s generation—the beats, and all that. Influenced by it maybe, but not from it. And I like you calling me, hon," she said, blushing a little.

"Okay, what about the ride? Do you want to come along?"

A weekend trip with a man I hardly know? But he has an honest voice and those warm, friendly eyes. And he always keeps his eyes in eye-contact with mine; no man-scanning my body. I've done worse, and I'll have my own wheels . . . .

"Leaving this Saturday morning?"

"Yes, around eight."

With a big smile, she said, "I'm in. One long day, or two short ones?"

"Let's do two; it'll be easier for you."

"Where do we stay? Do you know any places up there?"

"No, I was just planning on staying in any decent looking motel in the area."

"Let me check into it. I was always the travel arranger in my married days. I'll Google it," she said, reaching into her bag.

"Great, go for it."

She came up empty. "Darn! I guess I left it at the cabin. I don't carry it around with me all the time like most people. Well, I'll do it when I'm back at the cabin."

"Fine. But I have to ask first, are you over losing Bruce? I mean, if you're still hurting, maybe—"

"Hurting? No, I haven't *hurt* since he died," she said with a sour expression with the word hurt. "I'll find us a nice place." She smiled a sideways glance as they mounted their Harleys.

That's curious, putting that special emphasis on "hurt" . . . Oh well, I'll have to find a better time . . . .

Six - Possibilities

The ride back to the Starvation Mountain cabin was uneventful; Jim and Penny arrived in the late afternoon. Penny found her cell phone lying on the coffee table.

"I don't remember leaving it here. Too excited about going on the ride with you, I guess."

"Cell phones are a pain in the ass, but too handy to not have. Sure you don't want to give me your number?"

"I think I know you well enough now. You have to be careful these days, you know." She found a sticky pad and wrote it out for him.

"Great, we can talk Friday after work to finalize the trip plans."

As he walked to the door, Jim wrinkled his nose and, sniffing, said, "I smell something, like someone smoked a joint in here. Did you sneak a toke before we left this morning?" He asked in an "I'm kidding you . . . ." manner, but it did smell like marijuana.

"God no, I haven't had a hit in weeks. I noticed it too when I first came up here, so I've been keeping the windows open to try clearing the air. But it's been several days now, and the smell is still here. I guess it's in the rug and furniture. It's getting annoying; I don't mind a little smell of it now and then when I'm outdoors, but not constantly where I'm living. I'll get the strongest air freshener I can find next time I'm in Ramona and blast this place with it."

"And I think I smell another odor behind the grass. Sort of like something rotten: bad cabbage or potatoes, or maybe some old meat. It's very faint, though; could be my imagination. Did you clean out the refrigerator when you arrived?"

"Yes, it was empty and clean. But I haven't noticed another odor; maybe because the grass smell is so strong. Gotta get that deodorizer."

"No kidding. I don't know if Pine Sol would even do it. There are fabric deodorizers for pet smells you might try on the rugs and furniture."

"If it doesn't go away in a few days after I've tried that, this may be the end of my days up here. I'll go back to my condo down in San Diego."

"That would be too bad. I'd hate to lose you as my neighbor. I'll try to help you with this. Maybe we can find a deodorizer bomb to set off before we ride up to Cholame; that would give it the weekend to work."

"I don't know about that. My clothes will smell for months. Like those cheap things you hang under the dashboard of your car? Yuk! I'd rather try to work on the carpet—the one and only carpet in the front room—and the stuffed furniture."

"Sounds like a lot of work."

"I'm counting on you to help. Might be what you have to do to keep me up here."

"I'm in." Jim turned to leave.

"Give me a hug before you go," she said.

She seemed to be the best thing he'd run into in years. It was an easy embrace, as if they'd done it countless times before. Their body to body fit was perfect, and their comfort with each other natural and easy. He wanted to kiss her, at least on the forehead, but hesitated. She took the lead: "Are you going to kiss me or not?"

"I'm in." Jim said and gave her a quick, tender kiss on the lips.

"You don't need to be afraid of me just because I'm a biker. I'm still all girl, you know." He gave her a longer, harder kiss that she mirrored with surprising warmth. *She was all girl—or woman . . . .*

Jim happily strode out to his Harley, started the engine, waved to her, and idled downhill to the intersection with Highland Valley Road, Van Morrison filling his mind: *Little darlin' come with me . . . on the bright side of the road . . . .*

Seven - Cholame

A fence line at the intersection of two lonely, two-lane roads near Cholame, California.

"What are you feeling?" Penny asked Jim.

"Disappointed, and maybe a little depressed, too. I thought there would be more here. A little monument, or at least a plaque?"

"Yes, very underwhelming for a person who was such a big star and still has a huge, loyal following. It's just a bunch of stuff people have left: cigarette packages, notes on little scraps of paper, some magazine clippings and photos, whatever they happened to have when they stopped, I guess. It's like they just cleaned out their pockets and dumped the stuff here. The rain and winds will blow most of it away, which is a good thing, I guess. But it doesn't seem enough," Penny said.

"Only that pair of aviator sunglasses entombed in a block of cement suggests anyone thought about creating something to try capturing a little of him. And that's pretty weird."

"What about something spiritual? Do you feel anything . . . a little mystical feeling?"

"No, nothing. And I was trying to be open to it. I thought maybe I'd feel a little chill, like a cool breeze, or even my mind's eye having a vision of . . . something; a scene from 'Rebel Without a Cause' . . . . You know what I'm saying? But nothing here where he died. Somehow, I thought standing silently in this spot for a few minutes, I'd make some kind of connection. Crazy idea, I guess. But, all this junk is too distracting."

"That's too bad, you were looking forward to this so much. Maybe I should leave you alone for a while."

"No, I want you here with me. But, you know, I did sense something—a strange feeling—when we topped that hill back there and could see down here to where the roads intersect at the place of the accident. I knew we were coming into the space where he died. It was an electric feeling in my stomach and the back of my neck, like . . . that's it; that's the place. It was the same view he had of the road ahead, not knowing that within a minute or two he'd be dead. I was trying to put myself into his head, imagining what he might have been thinking in that instant before the car suddenly turned in front of him. Like, maybe: 'we're finally leaving that flat, boring central valley highway area and are heading toward the low coastal mountains and some fun driving.' Or maybe he was thinking about the next day's racing; you know, getting his race face on?"

Penny shook her head and said, "God, who knows? Or maybe he was thinking about how he'd played that last scene in 'Giant', second guessing how well he'd acted as a drunk, and falling over the banquet table."

"You know, the legend is that he actually was drunk."

"Well, I always thought he'd overacted that scene. Maybe that's why."

"Maybe." Then pointing up the road, "There's a monument down the road a little way that a Japanese fan had made up years ago. We might as well go look at it. It should have been built here, not way over there, but at least it's more than a bunch of scrap stuff left by the roadside."

"Your choice, James. It's your trip and your dream."

"Yeah, might as well check it out, now that we've ridden over three hundred miles through boring countryside to get here. What a shitty place to die."

"Yes, but I can't picture him dying in bed, though," Penny softly said.

"*Too fast to live, too young to die . . . .*" Jim whispered, his voice trailing off.

"What was that? Wasn't that an Eagles song?"

"Yeah, James Dean, James Dean . . . ."

The monument near a roadside cafe wasn't the answer to Jim's quest either. It was a strange, abstract, square metal sculpture surrounding a tree that lacked any significance either could imagine. Dean's name, and dates of birth and death, in block lettering had been attached to the sculpture—and that was it. The thing was in the wrong place, and the meaning of its design, if any, was a mystery.

"Must have meant something to the guy that had it made, but probably no one else," Penny volunteered.

"Well, at least someone took the initiative and spent a little money to do something special. Why didn't Warner Brothers do something? With the money they made from his films, you'd think they would have. But they didn't want him driving race cars, so maybe it was a 'tough luck, dude, you got what we warned you about,' response?"

Sarcasm filling her voice, Penny said, "But it didn't happen in a race! Jesus, who knows? Hollywood greed? They're all money-grubbing lawyers with no souls."

"Yeah, and there's no glory to be had in building a memorial out here in no-where land. It's all about eyeballs and butts-in-seats for those types," Jim said, shaking his head.

"I don't think this has turned out the way you hoped. Why don't we go over to Paso Robles to get something to eat and check into our motel room?"

Our room! I like that, Jim thought, looking forward to having dinner with Penny—and whatever the night would bring.

"Maybe you were expecting too much," Penny suggested as they finished breakfast and drank the last of their coffees.

With a sly smile, Jim said, "No . . . last night exceeded my hopes and dreams—"

Blushing, she cut him off, and said, "I'm not talking about that, silly. I meant the Dean memorial!"

"Oh, that. That whole thing was just to get you on the road with me, and then to make you feel sorry for me, and then to—"

"Cut it out. I know you don't mean that. And I wouldn't sleep with a guy because I'm feeling sorry for him. I don't have the time of day for 'sorry' acts," she said, using air quotes. "And I'm starting to like you."

"Starting! What happens after you decide you like me? But I'm happy to hear that; I've been there since we took that ride to Idyllwild. I was just putting you on a little, you know."

Ignoring his humor, Penny changed the subject, "Has anyone ever told you that you look a little like Kris Kristofferson? Kinda scruffy, but rugged and cool?"

"You mean like a lot of bikers? Goes with the spirit, I guess. You should know the last woman who said that ended up moving in and living with me."

"Uh-oh, I always hated being the follow-up act. What happened, if you don't mind my asking? I mean, it doesn't seem that you're attached to anyone these days."

"Annie and I drifted apart. I tried to keep it together, but when I couldn't get her to join me in San Diego, it was pretty much over." After a long silence with neither saying a word as they uncomfortably stared into their empty coffee cups, Jim said, "Annie's part of my life is over. She died in a freeway accident up in Silicon Valley."

"I'm sorry, I didn't mean to take this conversation to a place like that."

"It's okay, I wanted to talk about it . . . and I want you to know I'm not some creepy old, lost, ex-hippie, biker dude who's lost his one and only true love."

"I don't think that about you, Jim. You look wonderful, like you're in the prime of life. A little age, maybe, but wise with it. I'm no spring chicken myself."

"Coulda fooled me, Penny Lane."

"I'm liking you more all the time, Mr. Jim Schmidt."

"I'm glad you came over to my ranch that day. Someone like you has been missing from my life for far too long." He reached across the table to take her hand, saying, "Let's head back. How do you want to ride home; back the way we came, or down the coastal highway and through L.A.?"

"The route you picked to bring us up here wasn't too bad since we avoided the whole L.A. mess. But going down the PCH to Thousand Oaks is a nice ride, and then we can go east on the 210 to I-15, and down to San Diego from there. I hate the thought of going through mid-day, Sunday L.A. traffic on the 5 or 405 on a motorcycle. Jesus, it's a disaster!

"Okay, I like how you think. Let's do it that way." *And I love this woman!*

Eight - Raided

The cabin had been trashed. Doors were unlocked, drawers spilled onto the floor, furnishings moved haphazardly around the rooms, and closets emptied. The wicked deodorizer bottle lay shattered on the floor, knocked off the kitchen sink.

"Shit, Jim! Look at this place! It's been raided and searched." She broke into tears and stormed around the cabin in disbelief.

"Okay, stay calm. Let's just take our time and do a quick inventory to see if anything is missing. And don't touch anything. We don't want to mess up any fingerprints or evidence that might have been left."

"Okay, I'll try to keep my cool. But I'm not sure I want to report this, if I'm not missing anything. Mack can do that!"

"I don't understand that, but let's check things out and then we can talk about what to do next."

With Penny leading, they looked through each room, cabinet by cabinet, drawer by drawer, locating Penny's personal belongings. Nothing seemed to be missing. Nothing belonging to Penny, anyway.

"My stuff is here. I only had a suitcase full of clothes and some cosmetics I brought along, and a couple of bags of groceries I brought in. But I can't be sure of the stuff that belongs to the cabin since I've only been here a few days and didn't memorize each piece." Then, with ironical disgust, she added, "I don't see anything obvious. I mean, look, the sink and kitchen stuff, and the sofa are all still here . . . . What the fuck would I know? And furthermore, I don't care!"

"So, if they found what they were looking for, it's something you weren't aware of."

"I don't want to call the police on this, Jim."

"Why not?"

"It's not my place and I don't want to get into a discussion of who the owner is, why I've been staying here, and answering a bunch of questions I don't have answers for."

"But that's not a big deal. Your friend wanted you to use it."

"My friend is in jail."

"Jail! Mack?"

"Yes, Mack."

"What for?'

"I don't know. I'm nervous about it and I'm afraid of getting pulled into something I don't want to be involved in."

"No kidding!"

Penny told Jim the entire story of the job offer, Mack's frequent absences, and his call from jail. She finished by saying she'd insisted to Mack that she would only continue with the job and the cabin for a week or two if things weren't cleared up.

"And he said it was all a misunderstanding that his lawyer could deal with."

"That's what they all say," Jim responded.

"I'm going to get out of here—now. I don't like what's happening and want to pack my things to go back to my apartment today."

"Wait. How do you know this doesn't have something to do with you? Maybe they came to get you because of whatever it is that Mack is in trouble over. Or maybe this cabin holds a secret people are after and they think you have it, or know about it."

"God, I know. That's been in the back of my mind."

"Look, I am not allowing you to get deeper into something that could be dangerous for you. Your Mustang has been parked up here the entire time, so it's possible they know who you are and where you live. Come to my place and stay with me until we get an idea of what's happening and figure out what to do about it."

"Could I? Yes . . . yes, I want to do that."

"Okay, let's put the Harley back in the storage room, lock the place up and leave. But we don't want to put all this stuff back in place, or touch anything. We'll leave everything as is, but use paper towels whenever we have to touch anything."

"Why?"

"You want to get as far away from whatever is going on with this and Mack as possible. In fact, we should take some of those Clorox wipes and wipe everything down that we've touched."

"I still don't understand."

"You don't know what position Mack will take when he finds out about this. Will he shield you, or will he try to dump it on you? If there is no trace of you having been here, it'll be your word against his. He has a credibility problem because he's in jail for something serious and your word will be stronger than his. Believe me, we don't want to have been here unless we decide to say we've been here. We may want to be able to claim we know nothing about this."

"I'm not sure I understand that, but I think I like the idea. There's no harm in that, is there?"

"Well, it is destruction of evidence if there's an investigation. But it would have to be proven that we'd done it. The raiders might have wiped the place down it as far as anyone could know. So, I'm in favor of erasing all of our traces. We can leave the things we haven't touched as-is, so only the raiders' prints will remain."

"But I don't know what I've touched over the days I've stayed here. It might be almost everything."

"All we can do is the best we can. We'll wipe all the door and cabinet handles, furniture armrests, and the kind of things you're most likely to have touched. As for all the stuff that has been moved around, we'll leave alone, so the last, clearest prints should be the raiders'. We want most of the prints to be the raiders' prints. If there are a few of yours, it shouldn't be significant—unless you've been fingerprinted. Have you ever been fingerprinted?"

"No, why?"

"Because if we miss a print and the investigators find it, there won't be a match for it. They'll only be able to match your prints if they come up with a reason to print you."

"Whatever you say. Sounds like you've been through something like this before."

"Yes, but not as a suspect, more like as a third party. I'll tell you about it sometime. Let's get going."

Hours later, they'd wiped down everything Penny believed she'd touched, but it was a guessing game. She knew there had to be things she'd touched without knowing or had forgotten. It was a Hail Mary.

"Penny, we're going straight to my place. I don't think you should go to your apartment to get anything right now. We'll wait to make sure it's safe and that no one is watching or waiting before we do that."

"You sound like you've been through this before, too."

"I have. It's the story I said I'll tell you about some time . . . . Trust me."

"I do trust you."

"Okay, follow me in your car."

They found the driver's side door of Penny's Mustang unlocked, probably opened with the use of a Slim Jim or something similar since the door was undamaged. Except for bent trunk sheet metal, the car looked untouched. But there was no doubt it had been searched: the floor mats were rolled back and the console lid left wide open. The damaged trunk lid, standing open by a few inches, clearly had been jimmied. After Jim used a piece of utility cord to tie the trunk down, Penny tossed her suitcase on the rear seat, started the engine, and followed Jim to his home.

Nine - Shelter

Jim's house in La Jolla Colony, San Diego, the next morning

"That's my cell phone ringing," Penny said with surprise, as she and Jim were finishing breakfast.

"So?"

"Only a few people have that number, so I hardly ever get calls on it. It always surprises me when I do. I only use it for emergencies or making calls to people who are close friends."

"Maybe it's one of those friends?"

"No; caller ID says it's coming from the San Diego County Sheriff's Department. I wonder if it's Mack calling from jail?"

"This should be interesting. Are you going to answer it?"

"Damn right! I'm going to tell him that I'm out of his thing—whatever it is." She set the cellphone in speaker mode, "Hello?"

"Hey, Penny. What's going on? I tried calling you at the office and then the cabin with no answers, so I'm calling your cell."

"Mack, how did you get this number? I didn't give it to you."

"Yes, you did. Don't you remember—the night you were at my apartment?"

Embarrassed he said that with Jim listening, and knowing it was a lie, Penny wanted to end the debate. "I don't give my cell number to anyone, Mack!"

"Okay, have it your way; I got it from information."

"That's bullshit, Mack. Screw it, what do you want?"

"Why aren't you at Ramona?"

"Because I quit. There's something going on that scares me and I don't want to be involved in whatever the hell it is. I don't trust this deal, Mack."

"What are you talking about? What do you think is going on?"

With ice in her voice, Penny said, "Someone raided the cabin over the weekend. They tore the whole damn place apart searching for something. I don't need this, Mack. I'm trying to move on from my last job to something new, and I run into this? Fuck it, Mack! Where do you want me to leave the keys?"

"Wait, Penny. Not so fast. Can you tell if anything was taken? Or what they seemed to be looking for?"

"How would I know? I didn't make a list of all your stuff when I moved in, so how would I know what all is supposed to be there?"

"Did you see anything that looks like notes, or a warning, or clues?"

"Notes? Clues? What are you talking about? Do you think they would leave some mysterious, cryptic messages that only you'd know about? Or a note asking where the hell something is? I didn't see anything but a wrecked cabin. This is crazy, Mack! Where do you want me to leave the keys?"

"Wait, I'm trying to think. Jesus, I'm stuck here in this jail cell, and my brain is rotting away. Okay, let's do this. I'll call Gary and tell him to meet you at the cabin to pick up the keys. That way he can check things out for me at the same time."

"No, Mack. I'm not going back up there. There could be someone watching the place, waiting for someone—like me, for Christ's sake—to come back. Look, Mack, I'm done with this." Then, looking at Jim with a questioning look, "Tell Gary that I'll meet him in the front of the warehouse and drop the keys with him there."

Jim nodded his head in agreement, mouthing the words, "Good idea".

"Where are you now, at your condo? I can have Gary go there if that's what you want."

"No, Mack, I'm with a friend."

"Well, just go to your place whenever you want and I'll have Gary meet you there."

"No, I'm staying away from there until I feel safe. I don't know if they were looking for something related to you, or if they're after me, for God's sake! All I know is that nothing like this ever happened to me before I got involved with your 'businesses,'" Penny said, sarcastically.

"Okay, if that's the only way you'll do it, I guess so," Mack said.

"It is, Mack. Sorry about this, but I'm out! And tell Gary it has to be in daylight: make it twelve o'clock, noon!"

"It's too bad, Penny. You're a good person. I think this could have worked out for us."

"Maybe, Mack. But I don't need this in my life."

"Yeah, sweetie; I know what you're sayin' . . . . Goes for me, too! Be talking to you."

Penny furiously clicked her phone off.

"What's all this with the keys? What's the big deal with some keys to a shack on a mountain and that office," Jim asked Penny.

"I'd better show you." Penny went to the kitchen island where she'd left her purse and pulled out a ring of keys. "Here they are; must weigh five pounds."

"Jesus, Penny, there are more keys there than needed for a one door, two-room cabin and a one-room office and warehouse. That's enough for a small town!"

"Yeah, I know. He marked the ones I needed with stickers, but the rest are unmarked, and I don't have a clue what they're for."

"I've got a feeling it's those other keys that this is all about."

"Could be; there's a safe in the office he told me he didn't want me to try opening, and a special room he called a 'tool room' where he said he keeps some valuable, antique tools he inherited from his dad. He told me not to worry about that room, and not to try going in."

"I wonder if you somehow ended up with the wrong set of keys . . . ."

"Jesus, now that you mention it, maybe that's it! I might have a set of keys I'm not supposed to have. I think I should get rid of them fast."

"Agreed. Let's go up there later today to look the place over before we do the drop."

"Can't be soon enough for me. I'm worried."

"Okay, here's how I think we should do this. We'll ride up there on one of my bikes. I have an abandoned, out-of-state, motorcycle license plate that's not associated with my name I'll put on my fastest bike. We can't be tracked by the license plate, and no one will ever catch us on that bike. When Gary calls to set the day and time, you're going to tell him you'll meet him in the center of the parking lot. You're not going into the building under any circumstance. We'll ride up to where he's standing and toss the keys to him and blast away. I want to do it so fast that no one can tail us. I don't trust anyone involved with Mack and whatever he's doing."

"Okay. I like this plan—and that you're here helping me, Jim."

"I like that you're here with me—period, Penny. And one more thing, if Gary calls and wants to do it today, tell him no, you want to do it tomorrow, or even the day after."

"But why? I want to get away from this as fast as possible."

"Because I want to see what we'll be getting into. We'll drive up there today in my car and check it out. I want to make sure we can get in and out without being trapped."

"You're as suspicious of all this as much as I am—or even more! Why?"

"Add it up: Mack is in jail with a huge bail bond he can't pay, and his lawyer hasn't managed to get him out yet. He has this mysterious motorcycle business up in Ramona that's probably a front, and then there's his cabin on a remote mountain—that smells like a bale of marijuana—and has now been raided."

"I know. I just wanted to hear it coming from you to see if it's as bad as I've been imagining it."

"It is. How did you ever get involved with this 'Mack'?" Jim asked as he walked to the side wall of the adjoining office and, using a large skeleton key, opened the lower drawer of a massive armoire positioned next to a matching, also massive, oak desk. He lifted a heavy pistol from the drawer. "Just in case."

"I don't know. It . . . it was one of those *things*," Penny answered, looking despondent. "I guess I'm what you would call a 'middle-aged woman' with little going for me: no savings, no real home, no family, and feeling like I need to make a big change. You know, the money was good, so it was a grab at the brass ring kinda thing."

"Yeah, I can understand that, Penny. Looks like the grab was a big miss."

"No kidding!" Then Penny shivered and said, "I hope it doesn't come to something like that gun suggests. Maybe I should just mail the damn keys to him."

"I'd be okay with that. When the mysterious Mr. Gary calls, try it on him. In the meanwhile, I think we need to take care of ourselves," Jim said, patting the gun.

"Why do you have that? Those things make me nervous."

"Don't worry, Penny. I've had it for a long time. Back in my years up in Silicon Valley, working with CIA, ex-CIA, NSA, ex-NSA, FBI and just plain old ex-military types, everyone carried guns. They were all licensed to carry; it was like a club, everyone packing. We used to go up into the Santa Cruz mountains and blow up a ton of cans and stuff on weekends. But, I'm licensed for this and am trained to use it only when necessary."

"Well, this is a side of you I didn't expect."

"I don't want to worry you over it. I've never shot anyone; not even a mugger. Never had the chance."

"Okay. I'll think of you as a Roy Rogers kind of guy then: the gun is the last resort—right?"

"Never had anyone accuse me of being Roy Rogers before. But I'll take that to being compared to Gabby Hayes."

She gave him a little nudge with her foot and smiled, saying, "But Peter Gunn was kind of cool though . . . . Just keep it hidden so I don't have to see it."

"Peter Gunn was before you were born. Why do you remember him?"

"My dad loved that show and always wanted me to watch the reruns with him. The first time I heard that Mancini theme song with the pounding bass guitar line, and then the sax coming in, I was hooked."

"He carried a .38 Detective Special revolver. Easy to hide on your person and effective at close range," Jim replied.

"What, are you some kind of gun nut? Do I have to worry about you being one of 'them'?"

"It just happens that was my first gun. This is my second. I kept it because I learned to shoot with it. Sentimental, I guess. Do you want to learn to shoot it?"

"No, my dad taught me how to shoot guns and that was enough. I don't want them around me."

"Okay, but it could come in handy sometime. Look, you won't have to think about this one, I have a special place for it on my bike. Don't worry."

"Gary, give me an address I can just mail the damn keys to. I'm done with Ramona."

Gary's wet, gravelly voice, suggesting either a heavy chest cold or too many cartons of cigarettes, answered. "Nah, Mack's not gonna go for that. He wants to make an exchange. I have a check for one thousand dollars he made out to you I'm supposed to give you when you give me the keys."

"I . . . I don't know . . . . Why?"

"The bonus and back pay."

"Look, Gary, I'm worried about all of this and don't want to get in any deeper. He can mail me the check."

"We still need the keys right away. We gotta operate the business and can't do it without those keys."

"I can't do it today. Maybe tomorrow."

"Tomorrow then; nine o'clock sharp."

"I can't be there that early. I can make it at noon though."

"Okay, 12:00 noon; at the front door."

"No, Gary, I don't have time to stop and chat. I'll meet you in the parking lot at the sign board out near the gate and hand you the keys and leave. If you have that check, just hand it to me then."

"Penny, you act like you don't trust me."

"Gary, I don't know you, and there's all kinds of shit happening that has me worried. What the hell do you expect? We have to do it this way."

"Okay, have it your way. See you at noon, tomorrow."

Acting like people out on a casual drive, Penny and Jim looked the Ramona airport over from Jim's Porsche. They could have been wealthy aviators looking for a hanger to store an airplane, more interested in the airport and its ground support facilities than casing the dilapidated, corrugated sheet metal building across the road.

Amazement on his face, Jim asked, "Jesus, Penny, did you look this place over before you accepted Mack's offer? This is a dump! Were you out of your mind?"

"I told you; I was on the rebound and needed a change, and to tell the truth, I never gave what the building looked like a thought. Mack had always been a friend who I liked—within certain limits as I told you—and the idea of getting away from the constant hassles of my job in property management in San Diego for a while seemed like a good one. That fucking telephone never stopped ringing with someone pissed about something or the other on the line. I can't explain it, sometimes you just go with something that is contrary to what your brain says is the better thing to do. Tired of being Ms. Correct all the time, I guess."

"Yeah, but, this place? Look, I don't want to second guess you; I want to help you. So that's the office door over there at the front corner by the parking lot?"

"Yes. And way in the back corner is the big door that opens to the warehouse. It's almost never open."

"And what about the main gate, out here by the road; have you ever seen it closed and locked?"

"Oh yes. One of the guys, John, was always around the warehouse and would wait for me to leave, and then close and lock it with the control in the office."

"And what then? Did he stay behind after you left?"

"Yes. He was Mack's security guy and stayed late most of the time. There was a cot back there, and he might even have stayed overnight sometimes."

"So, the front lot gate works then, and it's always closed overnight?"

"Yeah, probably works better than anything else out here. It shuts very fast; darn near knocks the end post over when it hits. Seems like that gate working well was a high priority."

"Hmmmm. What about the big sliding door; same thing?"

"Yes, keeping things locked up tight is a big deal for Mack. Same thing, a switch in the warehouse closes it, too. There's something called a mag-lock the gate and the sliding door both have that makes them impossible to push open after they're closed; you cannot force them back open, even using a crowbar. But Mack's even got padlocks and locking bars that get pushed into place after the warehouse door is shut as well."

"Sounds like he's a little paranoid. Are there security cameras, too?"

"Oh yeah. Inside, outside, all around the place. There are twelve in all."

"Not surprising. That's fairly common with businesses today. Okay, so I don't see anything suspicious for us to be worried about tomorrow. The parking lot is wide open and empty except that sign. We should be able to drive in, toss the keys to Gary, keep moving in a one-eighty turn and drive on out."

"I hope so, Jim. Get me out of this!"

"The only thing that bothers me a little is what you said about how fast that gate closes. We'll need to keep an eye out for that. Someone could hit the switch before we can get out."

"Another good reason to meet out by the sign near the gate like I told Gary I wanted to do."

"Look, if he's not out there, we're just going to throw the keys as close to him as we can and leave. Fuck the check for $1,000. That's easy for me to say since it would be your money, but it's what I think we should do."

"I don't want the money; it's probably dirty money, anyway. For all we know, the cops are probably watching his bank account activity. I don't want to have to explain anything to them."

"I like you, Penny Lane. You're a smart lady. Maybe we should hang out more."

"Like we already aren't, Jim Schmidt . . . ?"

He smiled and said, "You're a fun person. I just might show you a secret dirt trail tomorrow that we may need to use if we have to give anyone the slip."

"Secrets! I love secrets and secret places. Do you know many?"

"Enough to keep you interested for a while . . . ."

Ten - Ramona

They took Jim's BMW 1600 with its comfortable passenger back rest, hand hold bars, foot rests, and a top speed over 150 mph. Both wore black leathers and full-face black helmets to avoid being identified. If the keys truly were the things of highest importance, Gary wouldn't need to see any faces.

As they rode toward the open gate of Mack's Ramona building, a single, large man was standing a few feet from the corner office door. The parking lot was empty except for two cars parked out near the gate. Jim suspected a trap: any innocent business-related visitors would park near the office door, not out by the road. But no one was visible in either of the parked vehicles as Jim drove intentionally near them, checking the passenger compartments before turning to head further into the lot. Penny tightened her grip around his waist as she noticed the possible trap, too. Jim had decided he should handle the keys on the logic he'd be able to throw them further—or further away—if needed at any signs of trouble. He had the keys in his left hand, keeping his right hand free to operate the throttle.

He stopped the BMW midway to the office building, still well out in the parking lot, and motioned for the man he supposed was Gary to come toward the bike. The man didn't move, instead lifting, and opening his arms as though he didn't understand Jim's meaning. In the same moment, Jim realized it was probably a signal and noticed movement behind a dumpster at the far opposite corner of the office. Someone was making a break toward one of the parked cars. Jim dropped the keys near the side of the BMW to make the man waste time coming after them, popped the clutch and, using the loose parking lot gravel to skid the bike in a tight, 180-degree circle, blasted for the now-closing gate. The man running toward the parked car didn't have a chance of getting to it in time and pulled a handgun from his trouser pocket.

Jim and Penny made it through the gate with inches to spare and were out onto the roadway before the man with the gun could get into a firing position and take aim. It could have been close—or worse—if they hadn't made the trip the previous day and talked it over. As far as they could tell, they'd gotten away clean with no vehicles following them.

Jim used shortcuts: farm roads leading away from the airport bypassing residential and commercial areas to get to the main highway leading out of Ramona faster. He wanted to be on the major commercial road that would take them back into the San Diego metro area and Jim's home as fast as possible. Riding much of the trip surrounded by the normal traffic on this route provided a measure of cover. Safety in numbers was his logic. It wasn't the most scenic ride, but it was the safest.

"What the fuck is going on?" Jim asked, not Penny, but more rhetorically as they sat at the kitchen island, sipping Jack Daniels on the rocks.

"I don't know, but the keys aren't the only things they are after. They want me."

"Yeah, I know. But why?"

"I don't have a clue. I guess they think I know something that I shouldn't know."

"From what I understand your responsibilities were, there are far more keys on that keyring than you would have needed. Maybe they think you used them and found stuff you aren't supposed to know about."

"Yes, I've thought about that too. But I'm also wondering if he . . . they . . . whoever, might think I saw something in Mack's paperwork they didn't want me to know about."

"Like, maybe something that has nothing to do with hard money loans, or motorcycle parts?"

"Yes. But God knows what it might have been. I didn't notice anything unusual."

"Look, we don't want to go on living under this kind of mystery for who knows how long. Here's a thought. Why not go to the jail and confront him?"

Startled, Penny looked confused. She gathered her thoughts and said, "That might be a good idea. We could tell him to level with us and call it off, or we'll tell the cops what's been happening. That kind of threat might just work."

"It's a bold move, but it might be our best choice. Or it could make things worse. Let's think it over and talk about it again tomorrow. Dinner?"

"Yes! Amaze me, my amazing Jim . . . ."

"Got just the place. You don't have to change."

"Lipstick?"

"Love you in lipstick," he said as he kissed her on the cheek.

"Just the cheek?"

"More, later . . . ."

"What do you think?" Jim asked as they finished steaks and fries in a barn-wood café in the outskirts of El Cajon.

"Good food for a biker joint. The atmosphere is a little too funky for me, but I had to get used to places like this when Bruce . . . ."

Cutting her off from going there, Jim said, "Yeah, you're right. But I didn't mean the joint. I was thinking about this whole deal you're caught up in."

"Oh that! I managed to forget about it for a while, being here with you . . . . God, I don't know . . . . I can't believe all the shit that's happened in the last few days—and it's probably not over."

"I know. And I feel like I'm taking over your life. I don't mean to do it, but it feels like there's some kind of . . . of convergence or something happening that's leading us both on an unknown path."

"Karma? Our mutual karma? Do you believe in fate, Jim? Like some cosmic forces resulting from our past lives have merged and programmed the future for us?"

"I'm starting to think so. I've always tried and wanted to be open to unknown forces influencing my life. Like . . . I was ready to experience some kind of force up there at Dean's death site. Ever since I discovered how closely his death and my birth coincided, and that my home was in the same county in Indiana that his was—a few miles down a gravel road—I've believed someday I'd find something mystical pulling me close to him. But, now I know I was wrong about that; I didn't feel a thing. I'm still disappointed about that."

"What about me?"

What about me? Jim slowly placed the drink he'd been lifting toward his lips back down on the table, staring into Penny's eyes. He saw an unassuming, honest face, unashamedly and unapologetically offering herself to him. *I don't deserve her, she's far too good for me. She looks like she's half my age!* Unable to say anything in response for an awkwardly long time, he finally said, "What about you? My God, yes! I'll give up all my fantasies for you. You're real, and you're here: sitting with me, smiling at me, connecting with me . . . . What more could I ask for?"

"Maybe I can satisfy your need for mysticism and dreams?"

"You don't know how good that sounds, Penny. It's been such a long time since I had someone. . . But this isn't the place to talk about it. Let's go back to my place—and I can kiss that other cheek . . . ." *Was she talking about marriage?*

"More coffee?" Jim asked as he picked up the breakfast dishes.

"Half cup, please. You know, I've been thinking about your idea about going downtown to the jail to confront Mack."

"And?"

"I don't think you should go. This is our safe place and you have to stay in the background. Mack and his friends can't know anything about you, and we need to keep it that way. To visit someone in jail, we'd have to make an appointment ahead of time, and that would give him time to have friends set up a stakeout around the area. They'd see you, find out who you are, where you live—and we're in big trouble."

"Well, the same goes for you. They'd trail you back here and it would be the same thing. You can't go either."

"I know. We can do it with a phone call. Appointments for phone calls can be scheduled if the prisoner is willing."

"Let's do that. But you'll have to set it up, okay?"

"Sure, in for a penny, in for a pound." Penny said with a grimace.

Eleven - The Plan

"Hi Mack, it's Penny."

"I know. What do you want?"

"What the fuck is going on, Mack? Gary tried to trap me and a friend out at Ramona yesterday. A guy pulled a gun on us when we were getting out of there before they could shut the gate to trap us."

"It wasn't Gary. Gary's dead. So's John."

"Dead! What the hell are you talking—"

Mack cut her off, saying, "What did the guy you saw look like?"

"A big guy with heavy, long black hair and a black beard. He was wearing sun glasses and a baseball hat, so all I could see was a hairy face under a ball cap.

"Can you guess his age?"

"I don't know, maybe in his forties?"

"That wasn't Gary. Gary's got grey hair and a grey mustache, but no beard. He was over sixty."

"What happened to him, Mack?"

"I heard someone shot him. Probably one of the guys you saw out there. Probably before you got there."

"So you already know! Well, who the hell are they? Who told you?"

"I can't say, and I don't know who they are."

"Fuck, Mack! What have you gotten me into? Are you going to get me killed, too?"

"No, Penny. They're not after you. You left the keys there, right?"

"Yes, we threw them onto the parking lot when we saw the trap being sprung."

"Then you should be okay. They were after the keys."

"I don't believe it. I think they were after me. Why else would they try to trap us?"

"I don't know, maybe they thought you were a witness to the murder. But they don't have any idea of who you are, right?"

"If they are the same ones who raided the cabin, they might. I left my Mustang parked up there while I was away that weekend. They might trace me that way."

"Oh, shit. I thought you used your car that weekend."

"No, I used the Harley. It's one of the reasons I decided to try the cabin out, remember?"

"Oh . . . . Hell, I don't know what to tell you. If they think there's a reason to know more about you, then you might be right: they might continue trying to find you. I don't want you to get hurt. Do you have a safe place to go?"

"Yeah, and I'm not telling you anything about it."

"I don't want to know about it."

"Mack, why the hell would they be looking for me? You must have a clue about it."

"You had the wrong key set, as you've probably figured out by now, right?"

"Yeah, it wasn't too hard to notice I had about thirty more keys than I needed. But those were the keys I found where you told me to look for the cabin keys."

"Did you open the safe, or open the door to my special tool room?"

"No. Hell, no! You told me to not do that, and I didn't. Are you telling me there are dangerous things to know about in them, and they—whoever they are—think I saw stuff they don't want me to know about?"

"Possibly. No—probably, Penny."

"Oh fuck, Mack! What am I supposed to do?"

"Go away for a while. Maybe I can get this straightened out."

"A while! Does that mean a week, a month, or a year?"

"More than a week . . . ."

"Jesus Christ, Mack! What a mess you've got me in. I may have to go to the police about this."

"No, please don't do that. I'm sorry. This should have never happened."

"But it did!" Penny screamed over the phone and smashed the receiver back onto the phone cradle.

Jim, after listening in on the conversation via the speaker phone, reached for Penny's hand, saying, "I've got an idea. But look, I'm late for a meeting at work. We can talk about it tonight."

A little glumly, Penny said, "Okay. Anything for me to do around here?"

"There's a nice Windows 7 computer in the office. The password is FERNBROOK, all in caps."

"Okay, great, what'll I do after I'm bored with an hour or two of that? What's close by where I can go to get a little fresh air? What about the beach?"

"Here are the keys to the Porsche; I'll take one of my bikes to work. I want you to leave your Mustang in the garage. You can go over to Rose Canyon and hike around if you'd like. It's a small forest of cottonwoods and oaks, with a little stream running through it with hiking trails. It's easy to get to from here, you can Google the directions. If you don't want to do that, drive over to Torrey Pines State Beach and get in some beach time."

"Okay, I'll figure it out."

"Right. But there's one thing I don't want you to do. Don't even think about going to your condo for your clothes and things. I know you don't have much with you, but we've got to do that very carefully. Okay?"

Moving close to Jim, so their noses were almost touching, she said, "Okay, Mr. Jim Schmidt. Whatever you say. I may have to dress without underwear until we do get there though." She kissed the end of his nose.

With Jim away from the house, Penny went into the office and turned the computer on, signing in with Jim's password. Pushing back a guilty feeling, she opened the Google search engine and entered: James Schmidt, San Diego, satellite communications. She realized she'd trusted Jim without question to that point, but knew it was past time to make sure her gut feelings about him had been correct. A blizzard of hits came back: patents, technical papers, and honors given by professional societies about things she had no way of comprehending. He also had recognition for work he'd done at local colleges, promoting high-tech as a lucrative and rewarding career. She could understand that. And nothing negative—although she knew she'd need to search court and police records for any bad stuff. *I'm not doing that, I don't want to go there!* At some point people have to begin fully trusting others based on their instincts and learned knowledge. She was well into the instincts phase and at the start of the learning part; the college student work impressed her. *I do trust him!*

Still feeling a little guilty, but gratified, Penny finished another coffee while thinking about a safe way to go home for her belongings.

The video cameras!

After gaining experience with video recorder systems installed at the various properties under her responsibility, she had a small system installed around her condo for extra security following a few home invasions in nearby neighborhoods. All she needed to do to monitor activity around and in her condo was to download and activate the remote viewing software the vendor made available to customers via their website. Installing it on Jim's computer and using her personal password would allow her to see what was happening on a real-time basis, or view the recordings for up to one week back in time.

Two hours later, she was viewing her kitchen, bedroom, entrance doors, and garage interior. She scanned the recordings back in time for the previous three days and found nothing concerning. So far, so good! The remaining issue would be the immediate area surrounding her condo: the common area shared by the entryways to all twenty-two units in the complex, as well as the driveway behind her condo that served the garages of the ten units on her side of the complex. *Time to call Sheila.*

Sheila was the on-site property manager for the entire complex. They were birds-of-a-feather: both experienced, tough property managers. They loved sharing a bottle of wine and horror stories common in the trade, commiserating with each other over tales of the latest flaming assholes they'd been dealing with. They related to each other on a level no one else could understand.

"Hi Sheila. It's Penny!"

"Hey girl, haven't seen you around in days. What's going on?"

"I'm staying with a friend for a while. I need a little time away to get my sanity back."

"What's driving you insane—other than the usual bullshit—that a glass of wine together wouldn't fix?"

"The usual bullshit. I quit working for George a few weeks ago, took another bullshit job on the rebound, quit that job, and met someone who's a rock in a sea of more bullshit."

"Honey, I'd like to meet that man. He is a man, isn't he?"

"Oh yes, he's a man! He's a straight shooter and is being more than a wonderful help."

"I like the 'more' part . . . ."

"I'm not sure I'm going to let you meet him, dear."

"Coward! Okay, but, you know this is all making me worry about you. Are you okay?"

"Don't worry about Jim. He's a highly-skilled technologist at a company over in the Silicon Beach area. He's a professional and a decent person. I know because I Googled him and saw his patents and awards and some things he's done for local colleges. No bad news, either."

"Okay, honey. But I'm going to worry anyway—and maybe be a little jealous, too, if he's all you say he is. So, what do you need?"

"I need you to keep an eye on my place. Can you have Tim point one of the cameras that covers the common area right at the front of my place? And, could you also have him point one of the driveway cameras at the back of my place and the garage door?"

"Okay, now I'm back to worrying big-time. I'll do it, but why? What's going on?"

"That new job I started and quit, you know? Well, the guy that owns the business is in jail. Don't ask why, I don't know. But some creepy things were going on that made me realize I needed to get out. Believe me, Sheila, I'm clean of whatever is going on. I just stumbled into something that feels wrong, and there are a few sleazy people I want to stay away from. I don't want to run into them waiting around my condo, so, I'm staying away for a while. But I'll keep up the rent and dues and utilities."

"Jesus, Penny! I'll do whatever I can to help. You know I think a lot of you. This sounds weird."

"It is weird. I haven't gone to the police yet, but I may have to. Look, I'll need to come over to get my clothes and things, but I want to make sure the coast is clear and that no one is hanging around my place—or the rest of the complex."

"Okay, I get it. I'll have Tim re-orient those cameras today and make sure we're getting good quality recordings from them. When do you want to come?"

"I'll give it two or three days and call to see if you've got anything first. And by the way, I have some of my own cameras that cover the interior of my place and garage I'll be checking out, too. You can expect to hear from me around the end of the week."

"Great idea. Okay, sweetie. I'm on it!"

The same day, later that afternoon. A rural, run-down adobe block house midway between Ramona and Santee, hidden far off Wildcat Canyon Road on a rutted dirt lane. Two men holding cell phones sit facing computer monitors in a dingy, small room with large-screen TVs mounted on every wall surrounding the two.

"What's Deep Tracker got to say about her? Where's she been?"

"Some place on Caminito Castillo, over off I-5 in the La Jolla Colony area. I guess the cell phone connections have been sketchy over in that area today, so the GPS is fucked. We don't have an actual street address. She was on a call to her condominium complex today and took a call from the downtown County Jail yesterday; both calls on Castillo."

"Mack! So I knew it; there's something going on between them we need to know about."

"Yeah, Carlos, we'll keep Tracker watching her cell phone. Keep paying the bills."

"Easy for you to say, Tommy, not your money."

Twelve – Proposal

Jim's house, early evening

"Hi Penny. How'd it go today?"

"Great. I've got something I think you'll be interested in."

"And I've got something I think you'll be interested in, too. You first."

"Come into your office and have a look." She pointed to the six camera views showing on his computer.

"Okay, so what's that?"

"My condo. Those are the cameras I had installed last year. I set your PC up for remote viewing. We can see what's going on there."

"No kidding! How cool is that? You did this?" knowing full well she had to be the one who'd done it.

Proudly sticking her chest out, she said, "Yep. You didn't know I'm a computer whiz, did you?"

"You're full of surprises."

"And there's more. My friend, Sheila, is the property manager there. I called her and asked her to have our IT guy re-aim two cameras so the outside—front and back—of my place, including the garage door, are covered with the association's cameras. They're on the recorder, too. We can check things out before we go there to get my stuff."

"That's brilliant! We'll give it a couple of days, and—"

"I already told Sheila that's what we're going to do. I'll call her later this week. She'll review her recordings—we'll do the same here—and if everything is cool, we go!"

"I'm liking you more all the time, hon. Okay, now it's my turn: Some people at work are setting up a going-away party for me on Friday afternoon. It's at the craft beer brewery near my office. I can't wait to introduce you to everyone. You'll love them."

"I can do without the craft beer: to damn hoppy and weedy for me. I'll be polite about it, but I hate all those crazy berry and fruit flavors they mix into it. Do they have cocktails there?

"If they don't, I'll sneak a flask of Jack in."

He kissed her full on the lips, and she squeezed him as hard as she could. "We just might get this thing worked out," she whispered in his ear.

"I'm looking forward to that."

"What are you going to tell them about me? How will you introduce me?"

"My cousin from Indiana?"

"That sucks! Give them the truth."

"What, that you're shacking up with me?"

"God, I hope you can do better than that!"

"My secret lady who's been living with me, unknown by anyone—even the next-door neighbors—for months?"

"NFW . . . means it Needs Further Work, sweetie."

"Yeah, you're right. I can do better. I'll have it by the time the party starts."

"Can't wait . . . . It better be good, our entire relationship may depend on it."

The trip to Penny's condo two days later was uneventful. Penny had been spending the hours when Jim was at work monitoring her cameras and talking to Sheila each day to compare notes on their observations, which showed nothing to be concerned over. There didn't seem to be any unusual activity at Penny's unit, and the same was true around the entire complex. Jim rented a plain white van they would use to get Penny's clothing and other items she decided Jim's home needed, including a few favorite pieces of bedroom furniture and small kitchen appliances that Jim didn't have. She left her computer there, running, so it could continue to act as the video-server she monitored at Jim's. They turned at least one lamp on in each room to give the cameras good lighting to work with. And they opened the shutters at every window for full interior viewing by the complex's security personnel, day and night.

Jim had backed the van into the garage and closed the big door for complete privacy throughout their loading work. Penny drove the loaded van back to Jim's place with Jim following at a strategic distance on Penny's

Harley, watching for followers. They were sure the move had gone unde-tected and that they were not being followed.

At Jim's they used the same scheme, backing the van into Jim's garage, closing the big, double door, and unloading in full privacy. Thanks to the video surveillance and good planning it had been a safe operation.

"That's a ton of stuff, let's drink to it staying here for a while. I wouldn't want to do it again next week," Jim said.

"I guess that depends on how this thing with Mack and his friends goes . . . . Or, you could make me an offer?" Penny said, placing her hands on her hips, and swiveling her body back and forth.

Make her an offer? He couldn't resist, "Like two peas in a pod?"

"You might call it that."

"If you mean a proposal, it's on the table, right now. And it's open-ended—no expiration date," he replied, opening his hands toward her.

"That was quick."

"I trust my instincts and always go with a positive vibe. And you give me good vibes. I feel great about us."

Penny reached for his hands, taking them both, "Offer—sorry, pro-posal—accepted, then. But what is it? I'm confused, are we talking about living together, or a wedding? I'm open to either."

"How about a wedding?"

"You surprise me, James, because at our ages we get to do whatever we want. But I'm for that, too."

"I need to do this, Penny. I really do want to finally be married."

"That's mysterious. Do I need to be worried about a woman, or something in your past?"

"No. Believe me, no. We'll talk about it when the time is right."

She leaned into his arms, "Yes. Yes, Jim, I accept your proposal to get married."

"Did I make the proposal, or did you? Seemed like it was you . . . ."

"I offered to allow you to make a proposal to me."

"Is that how it happened? I'm getting an idea of what debating with you will be like."

"How's that?"

"Challenging. But I like challenges," Jim said, kissing her on the forehead.

"James, that's not good enough after we just agreed to marry." Penny said with a sexy smile.

"Try this." He pulled her into a full embrace, with a long tender kiss.

"That's more like it."

"I can do even better . . . . What are you wearing to the party tomorrow?"

"I want better! How about 'biker girl'?"

"Does that mean jeans with crotchless chaps and halter top? I don't think so . . . . How about upscale business woman?"

"Pants suit and spiky heels? I have those, but that's not me anymore."

"Okay, so what are you, 'anymore'?"

"You'll see." *She was a long cool woman in a black dress* He couldn't wait.

Thirteen - Celebration

"Hey, Jim. Who's this pretty lady?"

Penny wore a trim, black skirt, hemmed modestly, but fashionably, above her knees; a sleeveless, low-cut turquoise blouse with a matching crocheted cardigan that reached below her hips, and low, strap-back heels. No stockings covered her tanned legs. A long necklace of black onyx beads dangled provocatively from her neck, sparkling against the turquoise blouse.

"Hi Steve, hi Ali. How did they get you two to come down off the mountain for this? This is Penny. Penny Lane. Penny, this is Steve and Alice Barton . . . or Alessandra Bertone, but that's a long story. Call her Ali."

"Hi Ali and Steve. It sounds like you three are old friends."

"You wouldn't believe how old—and how close," Ali said.

"Sounds like there are stories I'd like to hear sometime, Jim," Penny said, giving him a sly smile.

"I'll just say that Jim saved our butts once and leave it at that. That's a story best told up at our place in Julian with an entire evening and a bottle of wine, or cocktails, in front of us," Steve said.

"So, what about you two? You never mentioned Penny to us the last times we talked, Jim. New acquaintances?" Ali asked.

"Yeah, no secrets allowed between us—ever," Steve added.

"She's my fiancé," Jim answered.

"What? Wow! That must have happened fast." Steve's eyes widened.

With a surprised, slight smile of embarrassment, Penny said, "You wouldn't believe how fast."

"Oh, my God, I'm so happy to hear this! I think we're going to be great friends, Penny," Ali said, giving Penny a hug.

"I hope so, I'd love it!" Penny answered, with a big smile.

"And, Jim, I'm happy for you. I thought you were a committed bachelor and would die that way," Ali said, giving him a friendly kiss on the lips.

"It's not like I haven't been trying . . . ."

As the party wound down and friends were giving best wishes to Jim and Penny, Jim cornered Steve Barton by the railing overlooking the Japanese garden and fish pond next to the party's patio deck.

"Have you heard anything from Detective Daggett down at police headquarters lately?"

"No, no reason to. I saw a blurb in the paper about him retiring a while back. Why?"

"I'm not sure, but I may want to contact a detective about something that's bothering me. I sure wish he was still there. He's a guy I could talk to and trust with information and not worry about any blowback, if you know what I mean."

"Yeah, like not having something come back down on you if you just wanted some advice?"

"Exactly."

"Nothing to do with the Wu Tan affair, I hope."

"No, nothing like that mess; I hope we never get into anything like that again. I'll tell you about it when we can get together."

"What about next week? Can you come up to Julian for a weekend with us? We'd love to get to know Penny better. She seems like a good match for you."

"I'm glad you do, I think so too. This has happened so fast, I'm still a little numb about it. Spending time with you and Ali would probably be a good thing for both of us. I'll call you in a day or two. I think we'll want to take you up on that."

The sun was setting as the four sat in the screened-in patio of Ali and Steve's place, on Wynola Road, north of Julian. Apple orchards and vineyards surrounded the property, providing an intimate setting for the old friends to get to know Penny. They were working on a previously opened bottle of Jack Daniels, drinking the Manhattans Steve had mixed on the weak side to avoid needing to make a last-minute run to the liquor store.

"I can't believe what you've been telling me! The three of you were involved in a kidnapping, drugging, forced labor, and murder drama, and the whole thing ended with the crooks being confronted and captured in Hong Kong—and the leader killed by Steve?"

"That's right," the men agreed. Ali backed them up.

"You all seem like ordinary people!" Penny shook her head in disbelief.

"We were ordinary people. Ordinary people who got caught up in one of the most amazing crime stories ever to happen in San Diego. We didn't go looking for it," Steve said.

"This is making my thing with Mack look like child's play. I'm sitting here with three people who've dealt with murderers and international thugs. What do I have to worry about?" Penny said with a weak, half-laugh.

"Don't assume we knew what we were doing. We were stumbling from one bad move to the next. If it hadn't been for getting hooked up with the right people and some good luck, it could have turned out much differently," Steve said. "But don't think whatever you two have stumbled into is child's play. That murder at the warehouse in Ramona is no small matter. The good news is that you both were unrecognizable and hopefully—knock on wood—got away clean. But there has to be a dangerous connection between that murder and this Mack guy you need to be careful about."

Jim swirled the ice cubes in his half empty glass. "I'd sure like to talk to Detective Daggett, at least to get some advice on what Penny and I should do next."

"Maybe we can find him in his retired life. I'll make a few calls, if you'd like. That other detective—Dale someone, if he's still at SDPD—should know about Paul," Steve offered.

"Morton, Dale Morton. That would be great. Thanks, Steve," Jim said.

"So, what's next for you two? A quick wedding and honeymoon somewhere on motorcycles?" Ali asked.

Jim, in an off-key, one note voice, sang, "*Going to the chapel and we're gonna get marrarried, goin' to the chapel of lo-ove* . . . . We're working on that. We haven't talked about it much, but I have this old dream of taking a cycle ride following the 'Easy Rider' route. Maybe it'll be part of that."

"Oh my God, I remember you singing that song when we told you we were getting married a long time ago. That's just like you, Jim," Ali said.

"Wait a minute." Penny cut in, saying, "Here's how it actually happened: He said he was thinking about doing that ride after his final days at work, and I said, 'Can I come along?'"

"Yeah, that was the second time we were together." Jim said. "And now, here we are . . . ."

"Love at first sight, then. I know about that," Steve said, winking at Ali. "So, it was a mutual idea then!"

"Yeah, but she doesn't know the next part—yet." Jim looked sideways at Penny, saying, "I think the wedding will happen somewhere on the way; location yet to be determined."

"Oh my God, I love it!" Penny nearly shouted. "We'll pick some beautiful spot out of the movie and do it there. How cool would that be?"

"Not the cemetery in New Orleans, though, right?" Steve joked.

"God, no! Maybe one of those beautiful places up in northern Arizona or New Mexico they rode through? Like one of the old Navajo monuments? I can feel the ancient mysteries running through the ceremony right now. Maybe we can get a shaman to perform the wedding ceremony!" Penny said. "What was that Van Morrison Song?"

"See? We didn't talk about that yet, but we're both on the same wavelength! But the song you're thinking of isn't 'Wavelength.' It's 'Into the Mystic.' I can see it now: drum circles, pipe smoking, chewing a little peyote, drinking a little mezcal, and sitting up until dawn talking with the Creator and watching the stars . . . . I'm glad you're getting into the spirit of this, hon, '*Let your soul and spirt fly into the mystic.*'"

"That's it. But instead of Celtic spiritualism, this will be Anasazi mysticism," Penny laughed as she said it.

"An ancient Indian ceremony. How cool would that be?" Jim loved the idea.

"This could be perfect, dear. I was thinking of your search for spiritualism, but you're way ahead of me already. And I don't want to do a 'Dearly Beloved' kind of thing at this point in my life: suits, gowns, veils, bibles, and hymns . . . not for me anymore."

"Me, either. I knew we were meant for each other because of that karma we discovered up at Cholame." Looking at Steve and Ali, Jim added, "It's like she descended out of a cloud onto my avocado ranch up on Starvation Mountain one day. How do you like that for karma?"

Steve gulped, and changed the subject, asking, "Are you going to ride your cycles all the way from here? Sounds like a long, hard ride."

"I know, I've been thinking about that. Those first 500 miles, through the east LA-Riverside area and then the California desert are a pain. Been there, done that—too many times," Jim said, frowning.

"Why don't you rent a van or pickup truck to haul your bikes past all that? Maybe to Needles? You could relax in a comfortable, air-conditioned van, or modern pickup truck, and then drop it at a truck and van rental place for a week or two while you're riding the fun part," Steve suggested. "Then do the same for the return trip too—after you're saddle sore and all bowlegged and sunburned."

"What a great idea! What do you think, Jim?" Penny asked.

"Seems a little like cheating . . . not being true to the quest, kinda thing. But, you know what? Screw that purity stuff. I like it."

"When are you leaving," Ali wanted to know.

"Within a week or ten days if we do the hauling or trailering thing, I'll need a day or two to get that set up."

"And what about the wedding location? Can Steve and I come?" Ali asked.

"Oh my God, that would be great, wouldn't it Jim? If we do it somewhere near an airport, you could fly in. Steve, can you fly your plane that far?" Penny asked.

Looking a little offended, but trying to hide it, Steve answered, "I can fly to the east coast in my plane. It has a 500-mile range on one fuel load and a full electronic, all-weather navigation system."

Jim stepped in to deflect the conversation away from airplanes, saying, "Jesus, wouldn't that be something? The four of us getting together somewhere out in 'Easy Rider' land and having a wedding? I love it. Consider this your official wedding invitation, details to be announced. You two will be maid of honor and best man!"

They finished the bottle of Jack Daniels and went to a nearby winery that served Julian Mountain wine and steaks.

"What about Farmington, New Mexico?" Jim asked. "That's on our 'Easy Rider' route and right in the middle of a bunch of old Hopi, or Anasazi, or whatever they are, ruins. There are cliff dwellings and ruins everywhere. Farmington has a good, monitored civilian airport where you two could fly in, rent a car, and get a decent motel."

"That, or Durango would be great. Durango has a better strip that handles regional, commercial jets. But Farmington is right on your route, so we can plan on that and use Durango as a backup if the weather's bad."

"Yeah, I know. I used to ski at Purgatory in my wilder days," Jim said. "But the ruins and the shamans will be around Farmington and Aztec. We should do it near there."

The trip and wedding details were planned, re-planned, re-planned again, and then lost in the descending evening mist. But the four of them now had an adventure to share.

Fourteen - Daggett

"Hi Jim. Here's Daggett's phone number. He lives down in Baja these days, at Rosarito."

"Rosarito! Why is he down there?"

"Says his money goes three times farther. And he likes the people."

"Doesn't he think it's dangerous, with all the drug activity?"

"Says he knows how to handle it. He said, 'Been there, done that. Don't worry about me.'"

"I want to believe him, but, man—it's risky."

"Yeah, I know. Call him. He said he's looking forward to talking to you after all these years."

"I will. Thanks, Steve. I'll let you know more about the trip as soon as Penny and I have the details worked out."

"Hi, Paul. It's Jim Schmidt. Long time, old friend!"

"No kidding. Hey, I hear you're getting married. Congratulations."

"Yeah, I guess even old guys get lucky now and then."

"You're not old, and it wasn't luck. You finally met the right one."

"Karma. It's all about karma. But, what can you tell me about Mack Allen? I'm worried Penny has some bad people after her. Do you know anything about him, or what's going on?"

"Only a little. But, there may be multiple things happening."

"Like what?"

"Let's start with that cabin and avocado grove on Starvation Mountain. It has a history you and Penny need to know about. It was the scene of a murder that was never solved a long time ago. A woman who'd been shot was found in the cabin after a neighbor smelled something dead and called the sheriff. This was in the summer of 2005. The case was never solved, and the victim was never identified. The place's ownership was hidden by a bunch of shell companies scattered around various places in the Caribbean. Whoever owned it stopped paying the taxes after a few years, and it sold in a county auction. Mack's dad bought it, but died soon after and the property went to Mack, along with a warehouse up in Ramona. There were traces of marijuana all over the place at the time of the murder, but no inventory; it had been cleaned out. The sheriff's detectives figured it was a gang-related deal and kept their ears and eyes open for any leads, but never got to first base with it. There's so damn much drug stuff going on in East County, you can't keep track of it all. Even though they've kept an eye on the place for years, they don't have anything new.

"The drug story doesn't surprise me. I smelled weed everywhere. But, I thought it smelled like weed smoke, not raw weed."

"So, someone's been tokin' up there; not surprising. But it could be more than that, too, considering that place's history. What about Penny?"

"I asked her, and she said she hadn't had a hit in weeks. I believe her. She's a straight shooter, Paul."

"Probably Mack, then. Or some of Mack's friends. He has his own story you should know about."

"What's that?"

"Okay. He's in jail on attempted murder. At least that's the charge. I hear they amped up the charge to try to roll him into talking about some other people. They think that even though he's a small player in drug circles, he knows a lot. And that's why the prosecutor set bail so high; to keep him in so they can work him. They've got a little nickel and dime stuff on him, too, to help hold him."

"What's the attempted murder about?"

"He assaulted a guy down in the Gaslamp district and beat the hell out of him. Security cameras caught it and he was easily identified. They have a simple case to win an assault with intent to do grievous harm charge, but they're hitting him with a plausible attempted murder charge to try getting something out of him. But that's a stretch."

"What do they think he knows?"

"He's been suspected of being a mid-level drug dealer for quite a while, but they've never been able to pin anything on him. The guy he beat up was a member of a well-known syndicate that operates both in Baja and our side of the border. There had to be a drug-connected thing going on in that fight, but they don't know what it is: deal gone bad, money due, a territory thing, maybe other."

"Do you think this ties into the raid on the cabin when Penny and I were on a cycle trip that weekend?"

"Could be. Question is: Were they raiding the cabin to find something of Mack's and unrelated to Penny, or did it have something to do with Penny?"

"Yeah, that's what we want to know. Look, I believe she's straight and not involved in any of Mack's doings. But I'm worried they don't know that and think she's got something they want."

"Keep her hidden, Jim. They don't know about you, right? So, you should do like you've been doing; stay at your place and lay low. Or, take a trip? Get married and go on a long honeymoon!"

"We're going to do that, as soon as next week."

"Good. Where are you going? Can I reach you if I get more information?"

"We're riding our bikes on the 'Easy Rider' route, you know, old 66 and new 40; California to wherever we decide to stop; not sure we'll go all the way to New Orleans since Penny hasn't been riding long distances for years. We're going to get married along the way somewhere that we haven't figured out yet."

"How cool is that? I love it, Jim. That's keeping right with my image of you."

"So look, the only way you can get in touch will be by my cell phone."

Daggett scribbled the number on a piece of scrap paper as Jim spoke the numbers into the phone.

"Okay, take care of yourselves," he said, "and kiss the bride for me. Stay in touch, I'll keep nosing around on this. I've still got good connections at SDPD and the prosecutor's office."

Fifteen - Mojave

Mid-April 2013.

"Okay, hon. I have a full-size Dodge van with air, captain's chairs, and deluxe interior to pick up tomorrow morning. It has plenty of tie-down points to rope the bikes to, and ramps to get the bikes up into the back."

"Great! I can't wait to make this trip. Just the two of us and the open road. Penny smiled and sang: *"Get your motor running, head out on the highway . . . ."*

Jim picked it up from where Penny had left it, *"Lookin' for adventure, and whatever comes our way . . . .* I'd never claim we were born to be wild, but, *Like a true nature's child,* works for me," Jim sang in his one-note, monotone.

"Me too. But, on the mundane side, do you have us set up for a motel and van rental return in Needles?"

"Done. We leave the day after tomorrow, bright and early."

They were somewhere in the Mojave Desert east of Barstow, cruising along Interstate 40. Her feet on the dash, Penny asked Jim, "Will you tell me about your life in northern California?"

"That's not a short story, and it doesn't have a happy ending."

"We've got lots of time. What? Two or three hours, yet?"

"Yeah, probably. Why do you want to hear about it?"

"Because I want to understand the person sitting next to me who I'm about to marry. And you said you'd tell me about it at the right time."

"I guess it's as good of a time as any. But the story doesn't start there. It started in Indiana in 1955."

"So, start there, if you want."

"Just another Midwest farm-town kid story. Watching the world from long distance through binoculars. Everything that was happening was happening a long way off."

"That last part is true for most people. So why did you want to start there? What do you remember most? What was happening right around you?"

"Just like I said. I was watching everything from a long way off, even though most of it was right around me, in my own home town."

"What does that mean? What about your friends and family?"

"I always felt like I was an outsider there. I wasn't close to anyone."

"No close friends? No girlfriends?"

"I wasn't interested in their interests, and vice versa. And I was too shy to reach out and try bringing them into my world."

"Okay, oh weird one. What were your *interests*?"

"Science stuff. Building radios. Doing stuff with ham radios."

"Aha!" Penny laughed. "I get the picture: science whiz-kid sitting in his room late at night, twirling radio dials and trying to reach someone in Australia or New Zealand, or some other far off place. Master of the ether . . . ."

"Yeah, that's the picture. I was a tech-geek before there were tech-geeks."

"Ok, but I still don't get why you wanted to start your story there. It's not very informative."

"Because that's what took me into the Marines. They were looking for people with radio and electronics skills. The Marines brought me out here, and from there I went to UCSD to get my Ph.D. in computer science—it was called computer engineering then—and after graduation I moved up to Silicon Valley."

"Okay, so that's where I wanted to start fifteen minutes ago. Go on, oh techy one."

"I will. When I was up there, I was still, maybe even more so, a tech-geek with poor social skills."

"What's that mean?"

"It means I didn't date anyone or have a girlfriend—all the way through college and into the first years of my career."

"I can't believe that. You're a pretty normal guy as far as I can tell."

"It took years—and a special girl. After I moved up there, nothing changed. I worked long hours—which was a way to deny my problem, rather than a reason for my problem—and spent my spare time with other engineers. Some of them were bikers, and that got me into motorcycling."

More interested now, Penny asked, "What finally changed things for you?"

"I met a girl named Annie. Our chemistry just turned out to be right for each other, we could talk and I wasn't clumsy or embarrassed with her. It might have been because she had been a software engineering student at Stanford and we had things in common to talk about."

"An engineer to engineer thing: the romance of electrons and math and stuff? Where did she work?"

Laughing, Jim said, "You would say that. But, this is the part that will sound hard to believe for you. I met her where she was working in a restaurant up in the Santa Cruz mountains. The place was famous for its fantastic view of the San Francisco Peninsula and most of the bay through the huge window behind the bar. It was a great place to do a bike ride for happy hour or dinner."

"She was a waitress? This girl with an engineering degree from Stanford?"

"No, a bartender."

"Okay, waitress or bartender, what's the difference? A Stanford grad!"

"She never worked using her degree."

"That's strange. Why?"

"Money. She could make more money doing what she'd been doing to pay her way through college. . . ."

Penny cut him off, saying, "You're not going to tell me she was—"

Jim cut Penny off, saying, "Dancing—up in North Beach."

"A stripper?"

"Yes, a stripper. She didn't do the full nudity thing, though."

"That's what they all say. Pardon my skepticism, but I don't think leaving a G-string on would get it done in those joints."

"She said she did well enough that she didn't have to go all the way. She claimed she knew how to tantalize men so they were throwing big bills at her while she still had her bottom on. And she never seemed to be hurting for money when I knew her after she stopped dancing; she always had nice clothes and a new car."

"For that to be true, she must have been a knock-out."

"She was pretty, but I don't think that was it. I never saw her act, mind you, since that was before I knew her. I always guessed it was more because of her personality. She could charm the skin off a snake, and that's the thing that got her the job in marketing later on, after her time at the Bella Vista as a bartender."

"So, she eventually got into a real profession, then?"

"Yes, and that's what led to our falling out, years later."

"But hold off on that. I want to know more about her before that happened. Look, I don't want to be a skeptic, but girls like that usually have a money-honey, or do a little moonlighting for extra bucks."

"Not Annie. She was a straight arrow. I never saw or had a reason to suspect she'd done anything like that. There were no mysterious hushed phone calls, or unexplained disappearances. She told me that when she first started dancing, she drew a line where things stopped. Too many girls, some of them other Stanford girls she knew, stepped over that line and never came back. It was a road of no return."

"Hard to believe, but more power to her for staying true to herself."

"As I said, I didn't know her in those days. But she didn't hide it. In fact, she wanted me to know all about it. She didn't have to tell me, but she wanted to. We wanted everything to be open between us."

"Okay, this is a good time for you to tell me about your time with her—if you want to. But you don't have to, Jim, if it's going to be painful."

"Her full name was Barbara Anne Parsons. But she wanted to be called Anne, or Annie, because she hated how people—mostly guys—would start singing that Beach Boys song when they found out her full name. *Ba ba ba, ba Barbara Ann*, you know? She hated Beach Boys songs—California bubble gum rock she called it—and she especially hated that song: *take my hand, Barbara Ann* . . . and 'Little Surfer Girl,' and 'Little Deuce Coupe,' and all that. She even left the stage when one of the joints played 'Barbara Ann' after the bar's DJ found out her full name. She moved to another joint after that."

"A statement of her principles? Sorry, I didn't mean to be cynical, I just couldn't resist."

"I'll admit I thought the same thing when she first told me the story. But she was so serious about it, I realized she meant it. She was as serious about it as that line she wouldn't cross. She didn't want to be anyone's joke."

There was a short, awkward silence, Penny looking pensively out her side window before she turned back to look at Jim, "I apologize, Jim. You had a long and deep relationship with her, and I respect that. I'm not going to make any more wisecracks." She turned back to the window, seeing nothing other than empty desert racing by in a blur. *Why did I do that?*

"Okay, I accept that. I met her after she'd left that world one day when I'd ridden alone up to the Bella Vista on a beautiful fall evening with a full moon. I was looking for a quiet meal and the view out of that window, by myself at the bar. It was an unusually quiet night there. No customers at the bar, and only a few diners in the restaurant. Annie was the only one working in the bar, and had her back to the door, looking at that view under the moon. I walked in, pulling my jacket off and trying to hold my helmet at the same time. I dropped the helmet onto the floor, and it made loud crashing noises as it bounced around off table and chair legs. She whirled around to see what the racket was, saw me, and said, 'That you, Grace?'

Then she cracked up, and I cracked up, and after we stopped laughing, she asked, 'Anyone ever tell you that you look like Kris Kristofferson?'"

"So, she's the one?"

"Yes, the first to say that. You're the second."

Feigning worry, Penny said, "So she's the act I'm going to follow? And now I'm going to be worrying about competing with her *talents* from her dancing days, too! Can I compete?"

"Oh, stop putting me on. You know there's no reason to think like that."

"But those girls know all those moves . . . ."

"I'm sure we were very unremarkable."

"I was thinking you'd have some new things to show me."

Jim's silence made Penny uncomfortable, realizing she'd carried it too far. She removed her sunglasses, "I'm sorry for sidetracking your story, it was thoughtless of me to say that. I'll shut up and just listen."

"Look, I'm okay talking about it with you. It was a long time ago, and it's best to get all the questions between us answered now."

"Okay, please go on. I want to hear more."

"She recommended the Bella Vista Abalone with red sauce that night. It was the specialty dish that made the place famous. That started a routine between us that went on for several weeks. I went up every Tuesday evening and had the abalone with red sauce at the bar. She always waited on me, no matter how many people were there. We both could feel a natural, easy warmth between us. On one of those evenings she said, 'I don't know what it is, but I liked you the minute I turned around and saw your face that first night.' After that, I took her motorcycle riding around the Santa Cruz Mountains every Sunday morning, and then we'd spend the rest of the day together. She was commuting up to the restaurant from her apartment in Sunnyvale and hated it. I had been renting a house in the hills behind Los Gatos and wasn't enjoying the commute down 17 either. So, I proposed that I'd rent a house I'd found in nearby Boulder Creek and we'd live together. No commitments, no splitting rent and house expenses; we'd just live together as long as it worked for both of us. Her commute to work would be a piece of cake, and mine wouldn't be any better, or worse."

"That was a pretty good offer. Did she accept?"

"In a heartbeat. She wanted to pay part of the house expenses, but I wouldn't allow it. I felt I wanted to do it whether she accepted the offer or not. But I hoped and prayed that she would."

"Do you think she might have felt a little compromised, or 'bought' with that arrangement?"

"I don't, I think she understood that I'd do it, anyway. And she kept the refrigerator full of good things, the wine rack full, and paid all the utility bills. It was a pretty even deal, close enough for both of us to feel like the contributions were equal, and she really seemed to enjoy our living arrangement. We loved each other, so it didn't make any difference; no one was counting."

"Did you ever talk about getting married?"

"No. I think we were both afraid to go there. We both valued keeping independent lives with old friends and going out separately—or together. I don't mean we had separate romances going on—it wasn't an open relationship thing—but we didn't feel we wanted to limit ourselves to doing things we could only do together. We were both home and slept together every night for almost five years, unless one of us was traveling."

"That begs the question, what happened after five years?"

Jim lifted his right hand from the steering wheel, turning it palm-up in mid-air above the shift lever, "A guy named Jeff. He came into the Bella Vista once in a while to sit at the bar and hit on girls. One night when there wasn't much going on, he started a conversation with Annie. He found out about her software engineering degree, and couldn't help but notice her obvious magnetic personality. Jeff was a marketing type for a Cupertino software company and could see her potential as an attractive accomplice in customer calls. Penny had kept herself up-to-date with the latest in personal computer technology and was a power computer user. She knew her way around the operating systems and most popular applications. She wasn't current as a programmer since she'd never practiced it in the field, but she didn't need to be a functioning programmer to be the perfect marketing specialist."

"I can see where this is going. She took a job with Jeff's company and drifted away?"

"Yeah. Her commute into the valley for her new job was worse than mine, and after a while she decided she had to move in closer. We talked about doing it together, but in the end, she told me she thought our good times together were coming to an end. I'd suspected that was coming too, but didn't want to believe it. I didn't try to talk her out of it, I don't believe in pushing something that's not there."

"Maybe you're too much of a gentleman?"

"Maybe, but I can't do something I don't believe in. I wanted her to be happy, and I didn't want tension around the house because we were forcing it. That was also around the time I was burning out on the whole Silicon Valley scene and thinking about moving back to San Diego. Losing Annie was the clincher. I wasn't going to stay around there without her; it would have been too—too hard to deal with . . . ." Jim ended this part of his story with a wavering voice that he tried to hide, clearing it as though it was just a dry throat.

"Jim, I can tell from your voice that this didn't turn out well, and it's getting hard for you to talk about. You don't have to go on."

"No, I'm fine. I want you to know. But stop me before I start to cry . . . ." he said with a wry smile. Penny didn't know if he meant it, or was trying to be light hearted, but she suspected he meant it.

Jim went on, telling Penny more about his burn-out in the military contracting business, his decision to return to San Diego, and his futile attempts to convince Annie that the move would be good for them both—maybe even restoring their old relationship. He described Annie's hesitance, because she wasn't sure she could replace her new opportunities in San Diego. He also knew she was probably right. On that one visit, it was clear to both the relationship had lost its magic. He'd held onto a thread of hope, but—there was Jeff . . . . Jim glanced sideways at Penny to see that she'd again removed her sunglasses and was watching him intently.

He struggled through to the end of the story when Annie lost her life in the crash on the Bayshore, just when, after years of trying, he'd convinced her to come back down for a week to reconsider San Diego—and him.

Except for the road noises, there was complete silence in the van for the next several miles, both not knowing where to take the conversation. Trancelike, they stared up the highway, at the shimmering surrounding desert landscape and evasive mirages that offered no happy vistas to take their minds off the sad story Jim had just finished.

Jim finally said, "Penny, I'm over her. I'd been losing her month by month for a year or so after she took that new job, and I knew it. Her death made me wonder time and time again whether it would have happened if she'd moved to San Diego. Or was it somehow written in stone that she would die in a traffic accident on a certain day and at a certain hour? I second-guessed myself for years, telling myself I should have tried harder. Eventually I realized it was a fool's errand and the answer was unknowable, so I swallowed hard and accepted the reality. I'm not in love with a ghost. And I can't tell you how glad I am that you walked into my life that day up on the mountain. I want you to know I'm not carrying that old baggage anymore, and I'm open for you."

Tears filling her eyes, Penny placed a warm hand on Jim's knee and gave it a little squeeze, saying, "That was the best thing you could have said. I love you, Jim."

"Glad to hear it, now that we're getting married."

The squeeze turned into a hard pinch. "You know what I meant."

They both choked back happy tears and rode along again in another silence until a highway sign said, "Needles - 10 Miles."

"Do you want to know the strangest thing?" Jim asked.

"What, dear?"

Jim hesitated before saying, "Well . . . I'm having second thoughts about telling you this, now. Maybe I shouldn't say it."

"Oh great! You dangle a question like that out and then don't know if you want to ask it? You might as well get all your secrets out now while there's still time to . . . whatever—"

"Okay, that was stupid of me. But, I don't want this to put a heavy load on you. I don't mean for it to be that."

"Well, hell, Jim, try me. Just say it without all the drama."

"Okay, then. Annie died in that accident five years ago the same day you and I met up on Starvation Mountain."

There was a long silence before Penny said, "Ohhhh . . . . Oh, my God, Jim. I don't know what to say . . . ."

"Yeah, I know; I'm afraid you're going to believe I'll think of you as a replacement. But I don't—believe me I don't—and won't ever think of you that way."

"Well—it's not only that," Penny began, "But what if things don't work out for us? You'd feel like you've been hit by lightning twice and it just wasn't to be for you. And I'd be feeling a ton of additional pressure to not take us there."

"Yes, the implications are endless."

"Why didn't you tell me about this before?"

"It never seemed the time was right. There was no context for it before."

"I hate to think that I now have some obligation because of this, or that I've been scripted into replacing Annie. That *would* be a heavy trip and I don't want to think of us that way. I want the natural feelings you and I have for each other to take us wherever we're going."

"I hope we can do that, and I'm sorry I brought it up."

"Jim, I'm not going to look at it any way other than it was a coincidence and there's no meaning to it. We could have met the next time you were up on the mountain. And then what? No implications like these."

"Can you do that, Penny? I hope you really can."

"Yes, if you can, too."

"Should we just accept it as karma that's out of our control—and try not to look for anything deeper?"

"Didn't we say that before at Cholame: It's our karma?" Then with relief in her voice, "Here's your turnoff to Needles, dear."

"I love you, Penny."

Late the same evening at the adobe block house on Wildcat Canyon Road

"Why the fuck don't we have something new on her by now? It's been six days and there's been no movement since that last trace on Caminito Castillo?" Carlos Garcia screamed over the phone at the two men sitting amid computers, cell phones and tables covered with maps.

"Nothing. It's like she turned it off and hasn't used her cell phone since then."

"Fuck! They could have jumped on an airplane to London for all we know. Talk to that app's guy again to see if there is something else we can do."

"Okay, Carlos. But I have doubts—"

"Fuck your doubts. Make something happen!"

Jim and Penny checked into the Needles Ramada Inn where Jim had arranged a room for the night. The plan was to change into riding leathers in the morning before breakfast, and after finishing breakfast, drive to the Desert Truck and Van Rental lot where they would unload their Harleys and drop the van.

"This is our jumping off point, dear. Excited?"

She reached to hug him and answered, "Absolutely," as her cell phone fell out of a side pocket in a bag she was carrying trip items in. "There it is. I've been looking for that for days. Not that I use it much, but I've been wondering where it was hiding."

"Battery's probably dead. Your Harley doesn't have a cell phone charger, so you should charge it overnight in here. Do you have an AC adapter for charging?"

"No. The only charger I have along is one of those cigarette lighter plug-in things that's out in the van in one of my junk bags. I'll plug it in out there so it'll be ready in the morning."

"Good idea. Hurry so we can go to bed."

"Nice bikes, where you riding to?" Fred, the manager of Desert Truck and Van Rental asked.

"East, following the 'Easy Rider' route," Jim answered.

"Yeah, you too?" We get a lot of people doin' that. Not many stop in here, but a whole lot of them go by, wearin' those Captain America jackets and helmets."

"I know. There are even high-buck organized tours set up for groups. They supply the food, drinks, and sleeping bags for where Wyatt and Billy slept out on the ground, and even motorcycles if you don't own one. People come from all over the world to do it," Jim said.

"Don't seem like it's the same. Probably serve wine and cheese to 'em, too." Fred said, wrinkling his nose at the thought. "A little grass would be better, doncha think?"

"I think you've got something there," Jim laughed.

"What about you, little honey? Are you really gonna ride all the way to New Orleans?"

"My name is Penny. Glad to meet you, Fred. I don't think we're going all the way to New Orleans. I haven't been riding long distances for years, so we're playing it by ear. But, at least I want to get to Las Vegas, New Mexico."

"Why's that?"

"I think that's where the beauty of the western landscapes mostly ends. I don't think I want to ride through Texas and Oklahoma: too flat, monotonous and boring," she said with an indifferent look. "And too many rednecks," she whispered in an inaudible, low voice.

"Yeah . . . flat . . . except for the Needles over there," Fred said, pointing toward a line of sharp, barren peaks, to the north, "It's kinda like around here."

"We just drove a couple of hundred miles through flat and barren," Penny said as she pointed back toward the desert to the west. "Why are you out here, Fred?"

"Cheap livin'. And I'm a river rat. On it ever' weekend. Love it."

Penny ended the conversation saying, "To each his own. I can understand that."

"Park the van over there by the office door, and we'll finish the paperwork." Fred said.

Fred ran Jim's credit card and pushed the receipt across the counter for Jim to sign. While signing the customer line, Jim said, "We'd like that van for our return trip if it, or one like it, will be available in around ten days."

"Should be something available. What are your requirements?"

"Nice big comfortable seats and air conditioning," Penny answered.

"That's all we have. Can't rent nothin' else out here without those. Call me when you're a day or two out."

They ran through a simple checklist while their motorcycles were warming up. Hand signals for slowing, stopping, turning, caution, and are-you-okay, which was nothing more than the usual curled, touching forefinger and thumb with an upward head nod. They also made sure their helmet's person-to-person radios were set to the same frequency and in working order. They planned to use the radios as the main method for staying in contact, with the hand signals as the backup if one or both radios failed.

Turning and waving at Fred, then flipping their face shields down, they accelerated out of the gravel lot, heading southeast to the three parallel Colorado River bridges into Arizona a few miles away. As they entered the highway bridge, directly above the California shoreline of the Colorado, Jim radioed Penny to stop behind him as he slowed on the narrow apron alongside the traffic lane. Penny asked, "What's going on? This is not a good place to stop, it's too narrow."

"Watch." He pulled his cell phone out of his jacket breast pocket and held it up for Penny to see.

"Are you going to call someone from here? It's too dangerous!"

"A moment of symbolism; pretend it's a Rolex," as he threw it over the guardrail into the Colorado.

Penny immediately knew what he was doing: making the same symbolic gesture Wyatt had made as he and Billy left Death Valley on their trip to New Orleans. Throwing his Rolex into the desert sand was how he cut himself off from the straight world's time and schedules—and maybe even any concern for the rest of the world. It was a gesture of not caring, a middle finger salute.

As Jim started to flip his helmet face shield down, Penny yelled, "Wait!"

Jim turned around for a better view to see what Penny was up to. With a big smile on her face, she was frantically unzipping first one pocket, then a second, and then starting to unzip a third when she stopped, and in frustration said, "Damn! I left mine in the van."

"Do you want to go back for it?"

"No. That wouldn't be right in this moment. It's the same, anyway; I'm cutting the cord, too. I just won't have the pleasure of throwing it in the river like you did." Then, with a radiant smile, she yelled, "Yeah baby, we're heading out, just like Wyatt and Billy!"

Jim gave her a thumbs-up that she returned, still smiling, as they snapped their face shields down and twisted the throttles—hard. Van Morrison echoed in Jim's head: *We were born before the wind . . . .*

Late afternoon, The adobe block house off Wildcat Canyon Road

"What are we getting from Deep Tracker, Tommy?" Ferdy asked.

"Nothing new. The phone is still at Desert Truck and Van Rental, same as it's been all day."

"And that's only a couple of miles from the Ramada where it spent the night?"

"Yeah. I wonder if they dropped a rental car or truck—whatever they were drivin'—and switched to something else?" Tommy mused.

"Seems like it. Let's give it a few more hours to see what happens. Maybe it'll start moving again and we can get some idea of where she's going."

"Then what? What if it's still there?"

"Then we drive out to Needles."

"Oh great, Ferdy. Can't wait!" Tommy sneered.

"Yeah. By the way, when I talked to Carlos earlier, he said we'd be talking to Arnie from now on 'cause he's too busy with something."

"I think I'll like that better. Carlos's too much of an ass—"

"Yeah, I know what you're sayin', Tommy."

Sixteen - Rt. 66

R t. 66: two letters and two numbers: symbols of freedom for generations of American youth, or for others, a hope to replace lost hopes left in a rear-view mirror. Or the words for a new song a musician hoped would be the next hit: lyrics courtesy of mountains and deserts, rhythm provided by rolling, curving two lanes separated by a painted white line, and percussion courtesy of the rumble of countless, gleaming, deep-throated motorcycles.

They rode through western Arizona's windblown, sunbaked, bleached colorless villages. Semi-abandoned and forced into obsolescence by the newer, faster freeway, and overflown by airliners, the dusty streets slept as cross-country railroad freight trains occasionally rumbled past sleeping homes and yards with bored children and weary dogs. Appearing to be miles long, the trains inched their way across the barren landscape, now only to whistle at the forgotten towns lying by the rail bed.

Finally escaping the barren desert and looking for relief from the heat and dust as they rode up to the pine forests around Flagstaff, an old diner by the side of the highway beckoned. Penny said into her helmet microphone, "Jim, I'm going to burst a kidney if we don't stop somewhere soon. How about at this diner?"

"Yeah, let's do it. I'm in the mood for a burger and fries."

"Thought we'd never stop. My back is hurting, and I need to get off this seat."

"I was worried about that. Let's take our time here."

"Have a French fry, that salad won't give you the calories you need for this ride," Jim said as they relaxed in the booth's turquoise vinyl-covered bench seats.

"Okay, but just a few. Please slide the ketchup a little closer so I don't have to worry about dragging my sleeve across your greasy burger."

"Here it is. I don't want to see mustard stains on that pretty shirt. You can have all the fries you want before they'll show up on your figure."

"It happens before you ever realize it, dear. You know, I can't stop the thoughts of what happened when we dropped those keys off at Ramona from creeping back into my mind when I let my guard down. What do you think will happen when we return to San Diego?"

"I don't know, hon. Let's hope the San Diego Sheriff and the SDPD get a handle on it before we get back. We need to stay in touch with them to see what's happening."

"No cell phones, remember? We were cutting all the strings . . . ."

"Well it was symbolic and all of that, but we live in a different time than Wyatt and Billy did. It's a connected world now and we can't avoid it. We'll get new phones before we head back—but in the meantime, let's forget about it and have fun."

"That's easy for you to say."

"Well . . . what else can we do?"

"You're right, James; let's just have fun. I'm glad we're doing this. It would be much worse if we were just sitting around back there, worrying about it."

"Let's talk about something else," Jim said, becoming philosophical. "You know this used to be called the old Mother Road because it became the primary route that carried people from the east to the west coast. It wasn't completely paved, end to end, until 1937. Before that, it was a hodgepodge of dirt, gravel, and paved sections. If you were driving before it was all paved, depending on the weather, it could take weeks to go from Chicago to Santa Monica."

"I'm loving this ride, James. But I'd have gone for the railroad back at that time. Jesus, what a long trip it had to be with the primitive motorcycles and cars back then."

"Yeah, but now it's become a legend. It's in our national DNA. Kerouac, the guys in the Corvette, and then Hopper and Fonda . . . ."

"Is this a test? Am I supposed to say at this point: Oh yes, the novel, 'On the Road,' and the TV series with Milner and Maharis, 'Route 66,' and the hit movie of '69, 'Easy Rider'?" Penny said with a smirk, not really asking.

Looking surprised, Jim replied, "Ha, that's pretty good for someone ten years younger than me. I didn't know you had that much Americana in you. I think you're a keeper, Penny Lane. What about Steinbeck?"

"Oh, you must mean, 'Grapes of Wrath'? Read it in American Lit almost thirty years ago. Tom Joad and his family struggled with their old farm truck through here, going to California to pick fruit."

"Okay, you're humoring me, now? Sorry, I can't help myself, I love American history."

"I know, I can see that. I'll stop teasing you. Please go on with my lesson for the day."

"Well . . . okay . . . as long as you are interested. I was just going to say this: The Mother Road brought easterners to the openness of the west, the dust bowl refugees from Oklahoma to the land of promise and milk and honey, and in a final touch of irony, became the route of writers and movie makers. It's kind of sad: all blood, sweat, and tears for the early travelers who really needed to use it, and now it's turned into this mythical, romantic thing that has no resemblance to its actual past. Now people fly here from everywhere to spend ten thousand dollars riding it on rented motorcycles with gourmet food and drinks waiting for them at the end of the day."

"Okay, oh philosophical one. I need dessert, another cup of coffee, and to kill at least another half hour before we saddle up again."

"Take your time. It isn't too far to Flagstaff and a good motel where you can rest your back. Then on to Monument Valley tomorrow."

"I can't wait to ride through there."

A tourist motel, east Monument Valley, the following day

"That was a great ride today. So much better than yesterday's," Penny said as she slipped into bed.

"It was, wasn't it? And the best is yet to come."

"You mean tomorrow?"

"No, I mean tonight," as he propped himself on his side and slid his arm across Penny's breast, placing his hand on her bare shoulder. "What was wrong with yesterday's ride?"

"Well, I did like the part of the ride on that old two-lane blacktop highway through the pine forests as we climbed higher and finally got to Flagstaff. But the first part, after we crossed the river and followed old 66, was depressing."

"Depressing; why?"

"All those little towns with all the closed-up businesses and tiny homes on dirt and gravel lots. What does anyone do out there? Where do they work, how do they make a living? What do they do other than watch satellite TV? God, it made me sad to think of people living in places like Peach Springs or Belmont with their populations of less than one thousand—and that's rounded up. I saw kids playing in dirt lots! How could anyone bring children into that life? There's nothing but an abandoned old highway, the railroad tracks, a gas station or two, no medical facilities, and who knows what the schools are like or where they are!"

"Remember in the movie when Wyatt and Billie had the flat tire and stopped in at a family homestead? That was near Valentine. Did you see the population sign back there: thirty-six? Thirty-six people! No wonder that family seemed to grow everything they needed: they had to!" Jim said.

"Well, I'm sure most people aren't like that family—if they really existed outside the movie. I guess people drive that old highway every week to Flagstaff, or back to Needles whenever they need something. I don't know how anyone could ever agree to marry a guy who wants to get married and live in a place like Seligman, Arizona; population 456—if I remember correctly. If I'd been raised there and hadn't run away from home by the time I was sixteen, the first question out of my mouth to any guy would have been, 'how soon and how far?'"

"So, you'd like to talk a while tonight, is that what you're telling me?"

"Yes, at least for a little while, hon. I'm not trying to put you off, but I want to remember the beautiful places we've been through today. I want to hold onto them a little longer. They are special for me because we were riding together."

He kissed her tenderly, "Okay, I'm with you. What did you like best?"

"Remember when we stopped for gas at the same place they did in the movie, Sacred Mountain?"

"Yes. That was after riding through the pine forests and going up into a mountain area. In the movie, 'I Wasn't Born to Follow' by the Byrds was playing."

"If you say so . . . After we got gas, we rode along some huge, eroded old bluffs that paralleled the road for miles that then led us into high desert country. And then, at sunset, we rode into Monument Valley late in the afternoon. Remember the orange and purple and red colors bathing the entire desert? My God—Picasso couldn't have painted a landscape like that!"

"How could I forget? That's where 'The Weight' was playing in the movie. One of my all-time favorite songs."

"I'll take your word on that. I guess I don't mark events or points in my life with music—like you do."

"Sorry, I know I'm guilty of doing that. Sometimes I wonder if I'd forget half my life if it wasn't for the music that always seemed to be with me."

"That's odd. I've never thought about music that way."

"It probably is odd. I've wondered about it, too, but decided it's because I've spent so much time alone."

"What does that mean?"

"When two people are together all the time, something gets squeezed out of each to make room for the other. A couple will remember things by events they experienced together. A single person will remember events through other associations; for me, it's been music."

"That's a sad thought. I'd hate to think I could kill some of the things in you that make you who you are."

"Don't worry. I have plenty of space for you in my life. Now that I've retired, that space is huge—and you get it all."

"So now I'm replacing your job?" She teased. "I'm sorry, I couldn't let that one go by," she added when Jim's face looked troubled.

"What am I getting myself into with you?" Jim said, then smiling and knowing Penny would always look for the fun side of things. He loved it.

Penny lay quietly, saying nothing as she absorbed what Jim had just said. No one had ever said anything like that to her before, not even Bruce. Nuzzling her lips to his cheek, she whispered, "I told you in the van yesterday that you'd said the best thing that anyone ever could. I was wrong, this was even better." She softly kissed his cheek.

Jim rolled his head across the pillow so they were face to face, lips touching.

"And then you said you loved me. Now it's my turn; I love you, Jim Schmidt. And I've changed my mind; we can talk about today's ride tomorrow—at breakfast . . . ."

"Want to know the song that's in my head now?"

"Are you going to do this all the time? But I'm sorry, I said I didn't want to squeeze who you are out of you . . . what is it?"

"Van Morrison: 'Queen of the Slipstream': *And I want to rock your Gypsy soul* . . . ."

"I can dig that. Rock *me*, dear . . . ." Penny whispered.

Needles, California

"What a hellhole! It's ten at night and it's still over ninety degrees. Why the fuck does anyone want to live in Needles?"

"Rent's cheap?"

"Yeah, but what about all the electricity you'd have to burn tryin' to stay cool? Has to cost a fortune to run air conditioners all the time."

"I don't know and I don't care. What I care about is finding that cell phone and then her. We have to take care of Carlos's business."

"Yeah, but do you really think they're taking that notebook with them? Why would they have it out here?"

"Who knows, maybe they have a safe place somewhere along the river."

"And another question is: do they know what the notebook is all about?"

"You have too many questions, Tommy. Our job is to find them and get the notebook—or find out where it is—no matter what we have to do."

"What are we fuckin' doin'? I'm getting tired of this business."

"Yeah, I know what you mean. And some of the things we have to do . . . ."

Seventeen - Inspiration

The tourist motel coffee shop, east Monument Valley

"It wasn't about the keys."

"Then what was it about?"

"I was having trouble sleeping last night, and this mystery with Mack and Gary and whoever the others are bothered me. I think the men at the Ramona warehouse were looking for more than those keys. The keys may have meant nothing, otherwise they would have let us out of there without trying to trap us."

"Yeah, well, I think we already figured that out. So, do you think you know what they really were after?"

"Maybe. When I was working from my condo, before Mack had the Ramona office ready, I had this pile of papers and a few notebooks Mack gave me to organize his hard money loan data. There was a thin notebook—a three-ring binder—of pages that looked like maps; color coded maps. Each page was in its own clear plastic protector. I didn't have time to spend trying to figure out what they were, and they didn't look like they had anything to do with the loans, so I put the notebook in a pile of miscellaneous paperwork on a side table next to my desk. I forgot all about the maps until last night."

"What made you think of the notebook? Do you think it relates to the cabin raid and the murder in Ramona?"

"I don't know. But let me tell you what I remember and see if you have any ideas."

"Okay, do you want to order more coffee first? Farmington, our next stop, is only two or three hours' ride, so we don't have to hurry."

"Yes, let's take a little time with this."

With a fresh pot of coffee on the table, Penny continued, "I knew back then what the maps were, but they seemed insignificant. But here's what hit me last night. They were zip code maps of San Diego County. No big thing, right? But each zip code area had a different color. There were only a few colors used for all the zip codes. Like, there were blue zips, yellow zips, red zips, and so on; maybe six or eight colors in total. It was as though the zip codes were each being assigned to one of the few colors as though they belonged to something—or someone."

"Hmmmm; assigned to someone . . . ."

"Yes. And I also noticed there were letters—in pairs—hand printed in each of the zips. Like, for example: AR, or BM, or PS, like that. Like someone's initials."

"Whoa! Like the zip code area belonged to someone? Like a sales territory?"

"Yes. Like a sales area map."

"Holy cow! Do you know what I'm thinking?"

"That they're drug gang maps?"

"Jesus, yes! What else do you remember?"

"There were multiple versions of the maps, where each zip code might have a different color and initials for the same zip code from the previous map."

"Like a different map for each drug type? One map for marijuana, another for crack, another for methamphetamine, and another for speed; like that?"

"That's what I'm thinking. The colors correspond to different gangs; red is for one gang, yellow is another, and so on."

"In other words, the gang that has grass in one zip code might not have it for crack because some other gang has it for that, and so on. And that's why there are multiple maps."

"Yes, that's what I think."

"So, the set of maps is the complete definition of who has what for the entire county. What do you think that would be worth?"

"Dead people?"

"Yes, dead people. Was there anything else?"

"Yes, there were a few more pages at the back that I mostly ignored. But I do remember something about them, something that may tie everything together."

"What?"

"A big list of names. Dozens of them. Each name indexed to a pair of letters. I'm making this up as an example, but AR would be indexed to Antonio Regino. Like that."

"Christ! So, the index may give the names of each dealer or contact person, for each drug for each zip code?"

"I think so. And there was even one more for what I think was a reference list for the individual maps. It was a short list, done in a kind of crypto-scheme that designated each map. It was simple: what I believe was a map number indexed to a drug type. Map 1—and each map had a number in the lower right corner—was indexed to something identified as Gold. Maybe Columbia Gold marijuana, and map 2 could have been another type of marijuana, and so on. I couldn't identify the drug for each code, but I bet your friend Daggett could."

"You must have spent the whole night thinking about this. Did you get any sleep?"

"Enough. I might have spent an hour or two thinking it through, and then decided, I'm with the best guy I've ever known—think about him. So I went back to sleep."

"Was that when you put your arm around me?"

"I didn't know you were awake. Yes, I wanted to hold you."

"It felt really nice, Penny. You make my day, every day we spend together."

She lifted his hand off the table and kissed it, "No, *you* make *my* day every day we're together."

"Okay, we need to decide if we should rent the room for another day, or get on our bikes and see more 'Easy Rider' territory," Jim said, and laughed.

"Let's ride. We've got the rest of our lives to spend in bed, James dear."

"Agreed. And we need to think about what to do with this information. It might have something to do with Mack being in jail, and all the other shit that's been happening."

"I know. I think we should have cell phones."

"We're going to fix that. We'll buy new ones at the first place we find selling them."

"Where do you think that'll be, out in this remote area?"

"Probably Farmington. Other than going back to Flagstaff, it's the only city big enough within hundreds of miles."

"Yes, that's likely true. But I may not need one, I might still have mine. We should call Fred back at Desert Truck and Van Rental to see if he found it."

"Good idea. Let's head out. We'll be in Farmington by early afternoon."

Eighteen – Revelation

"My cell phone is at the bottom of the Colorado River—back in California. You can deactivate that one and activate this new one using the same number and account. And as soon as you've finished that, I need to use it to make a call. We may need to buy another phone."

After five minutes of calls and entering codes in Jim's new phone, the salesman handed it to him, saying, "All yours. You can make your call."

Jim called information to get the number for Desert Trucks and Vans and punched it into his new phone. "Hi Fred, this is Jim Schmidt. Penny and I dropped a white Dodge van with you three days ago and unloaded our motorcycles. Do you remember us?"

"Yeah, sure. You and that sweetie of yours were heading east on the 'Easy Rider' route. How's it going?"

"Great, we're having a very cool ride. Saw some wonderful scenery and beautiful places yesterday."

"Yeah, where are you now?"

"We're in a Farmington, buying new cell phones—which is why I called: Penny thinks she left her cell phone in the van. It's in a mar-bled-green colored case and was plugged into the 12-volt outlet in the rear console. We're wondering if you've found it."

"That's strange, Jim. Two guys were in here early yesterday asking about a phone belonging to a Penny Lane. One of them said he's Penny's brother and lives right around here, and that she'd asked him to come in to check on it."

"Oh, fuck! That's bullshit, Fred. What happened? What did you tell them?"

"I told them I couldn't help them. I said that I wouldn't confirm whether it was here or not, and that even if it was here, I wouldn't turn it over to them without hearing from the owner."

"That's great. So, what happened then?"

"They got kinda threatening and talked about how critical it was for them to know if the phone was here. I said, 'Look, come back with the police or someone with the authority to talk about it, and I'd cooperate.' Then they backed off a little and asked if I could give them any idea of where the person who owned the phone had gone, which was kind of crazy to ask after they'd told me Penny had asked them to check on her phone. Seems like they'd know where she is."

"Yeah, that's a crappy cover story. It doesn't hang together."

"The whole thing was fishy. So, to try getting them out of here, I told them that most of the rentals have been to locals, but I'd overheard two people who'd dropped off a van talking about traveling east on the old Route 66 and maybe finding some of the 'Easy Rider' movie shooting locations. But I didn't mention no names, and I didn't verify that a Penny had been in here."

"How'd that work? Did it satisfy them?"

"Not really. They said they wanted more information and got in my face again. And just then, two of my mechanics came in from the shop to talk about a returned truck that had some bad problems. They're big, tough-looking guys who you know right away are people you don't want to cross. I gave them a warning look and then shifted my glance over to these two strangers that signaled my guys to be on the alert. The strangers saw me doing this and realized it wasn't a good idea to press the issue any farther."

"Too bad you told them about 'Easy Rider' trippers, but I understand that you had to give them something plausible to get them out. What happened then?"

"They left, driving a large, white SUV. I think it was a Lincoln Navigator. They said they'd like to come back to talk again sometime. I think it was meant as a threat, or warning. I don't think I gave them enough to start them after you though; it was pretty flimsy. Oh, and I didn't tell them you were riding motorcycles. I didn't want to give them any more."

"Ahhhh, great! They'll probably be looking for two people in a car."

"Yeah, that's what I'm thinking. Oh, and by the way, I do have Penny's phone here. It's in my safe."

"You're a good man, Fred. We'll see you when we come in to pick up a van to take back to San Diego."

"Okay, take care. But be on the lookout for a white Lincoln SUV. And take good care of that little honey of yours."

"Thanks, Fred."

"Salesman, we need another phone, with a new number. And add it to my account."

Penny looked at Jim with a questioning face, saying, "So does he have my phone—do I still have a phone?"

"Yes, but you don't want to use it again, there is something suspicious going on. We'll pick it up on the way back."

"What do you mean, suspicious?"

"How do you think two guys would know to drive to Fred's business—in Needles California—and ask about your phone?"

"Some kind of GPS app?"

"Yeah, they're called trackers. Trackers can get downloaded onto people's phones without them ever knowing it. Someone might be tracking us."

The salesman handed Penny her new phone, gave her the new number, and thanked them for their business.

As they started their motorcycles, Jim said to Penny, "We've been loafing along, not in any hurry, but we have to assume whoever is tracking us, is, or has, someone following us. And they are probably driving faster than we've been. They may be less than a day behind us."

"We need to be careful then. So where to, now?"

"I want to go north a little way to Aztec. It's off the 'Easy Rider' route, but there's a ruin I'd like to see there. It's supposed to have a large, intact Great Kiva. Maybe it's the place we'll get married if we can find a shaman to do it."

"Can we stop for lunch first? It's past two and I'm famished."

"Sure, hon, I'm sorry. I focused so much on finding a place to get cell phones that I forgot about the time."

"Do you want to abandon this trip and take a different route back to San Diego to avoid the possibility of running into those thugs if they are actually chasing us?" Jim asked Penny after they'd settled into a booth in the Old Farmington Cafe.

"I'd hate to do that. I'm happy being on this trip with you and I'd never forgive myself for quitting. We can avoid them, can't we? They don't have my phone to track anymore, if that's what they were doing. They don't know we're on motorcycles and they don't know what you look like, and maybe even me. Neither of us has ever been face to face with any of them."

"That we know of . . . . Yes, those things are all in our favor, but we haven't talked about the possibility they tracked your phone when you were at my house. If they did, then they can get my address, my name, and maybe a little information about me—like that I'm a motorcyclist—or even your or my driver's license photos."

"Could they do that?"

"Yes, if they're good, and have contacts—sure they could."

"We should assume they've got the info on you then, don't you think?"

"We have to."

"But that doesn't mean I want to change my mind about going on with the trip. This is a huge country and it would be like looking for a needle in a haystack."

"A man and a woman riding motorcycles through this rural country are sure to be noticed. We'll stick out like—Wyatt and Billy."

"Oh shit, that's true. Look, I won't let my hair hang out under my helmet; I'll keep it all rolled up in there. And I won't wear makeup, I'll keep my helmet on all the time, and I'll let you do all the talking. I think we can look like two guys."

"Might work. But you're still going to be Penny Lane in our room."

"That's easy. I'm not losing my femininity over this."

"We're heading straight back to San Diego if I see any signs of it. I won't have it," Jim joked.

"You won't have it? I'd do it if I needed to, you know. Don't challenge me."

"Sorry, I guess I touched a nerve. I didn't mean that I wanted to control who you are. In my stupid way, I was just saying I want you to stay like you are."

"I know. I guess I slipped back into the tough old shell I had to put on daily to live in the job I used to have. 'Shields up', and all that. I'm sorry."

Jim hadn't seen that toughness in Penny before—her short-fuse defensiveness. But thinking about what he knew she had to put up with, day after day, he understood. He also realized it had to be a good thing; a woman needs to have survival instincts and ways of handling herself.

"Okay then, we press on?" Jim asked.

"Yes. I want to keep going."

As they ate their New Mexico Cowboy's Delight lunch of ribs, baked potatoes, beans, and roasted corn, Penny asked, "How would a tracker get installed on my phone? I haven't lost it—before the other day back in Needles."

"Leave it unattended somewhere? Like at a bar while you went to the restroom?"

"Oh, come on, you know a woman never goes to a restroom without her purse—which is where my cell phone lives!"

"It was just an example. It's the kind of thing that happens all the time."

"Yes, but the person who wanted to load the tracker on my phone would literally have to be following me around, waiting for the opportunity."

"Yes, that's the thing that's hard to believe. Why would someone have been targeting you? Unless . . . ."

"Unless what?"

"Unless you left it in a place you thought was safe for a while."

"My condo? I doubt it, the place has good security. But here's something to consider."

"What's that?" Jim asked.

"The cabin. Remember I left the phone there the day we rode to Idyllwild? It was there all day. I locked the cabin, but who knows who else has keys for it?"

"Jesus, you're right!"

They were both silent for a short while, thinking of the ramifications of what they might have just discovered.

Then Jim said, "If that's when someone installed the tracker, they'd have known where you were when we rode up to Cholame later. And with us three hundred miles away, they'd know they'd have plenty to time to hit the cabin."

"This sounds like how it happened," Penny said, throwing her head back against the booth's high back. "But we still don't know what they're looking for—unless it is that area code notebook."

"Penny, I have to ask you a personal question. Please don't get mad at me for asking it, but it needs to be asked."

Fidgeting a little, Penny said, "What is it?"

"I think you spent a night with Mack, if I understood that phone conversation when he first called you at my place. If that's true, that also could have been where the tracker got installed."

Penny pursed her lips, swallowed, and said, "That's true, Jim. I did spend the night with him. And, I'll admit it, it could have happened then. But, please don't—"

Jim cut her off, saying, "You don't have to explain anything to me. You're a mature woman and you can live your life as you want. I'm not bothered by it. I like the way you handle yourself and your life; that's why we're here together."

"I feel stupid, I . . . I want you to know . . . I . . . don't have any interest in him. He's an old flame that turned up at a weak moment when I just didn't give a damn, and—"

"Stop. I didn't bring him up because I want you to feel you owe me something—an explanation—or an apology. I only wanted to suggest that Mack could be behind all this tracking stuff—and maybe more."

Looking glum, Penny stared at the table before saying, "Jim, I'm never going to forgive myself if I did something dumb and you get hurt because of it."

"Look, I'll take my chances with you any day. You're worth everything I've got," Jim said, taking her hand.

Choking back tears, Penny answered, "Thank you. You always find the right thing to say when I need it." After a short silence, she wiped her eyes, "Okay, then . . . now what?"

"Time to call Daggett."

But Van Morrison was in his mind as he punched the numbers in his cell phone: *She's as sweet as Tupelo Honey . . . .*

"Jim, the important thing is to get that notebook as soon as possible. I'll get in touch with SDPD, fill them in on this, and push them to get over to Penny's place to recover it," Daggett said.

"What do you think they should do then?"

"It's not my call, but I'm going to try to convince them they need to think of the danger you and Penny are in every moment the bad guys continue to think she has it or knows where it is. I think they should call a press conference, announce the discovery, and that they have the notebook. That way you and Penny should be off the hook since there's no use for them to continue chasing you."

"Maybe they'll believe she made copies and will still want to take the copies—and her—out of play."

"That's why the police need to announce they have it. Once it's widely known SDPD has all that information, copies are irrelevant. When the drug dealers in those networks learn their cover has been blown, entire networks will fall apart. No one is going to deal with others for fear of being caught dealing. They'll know the cops will be staking out and watching all those names like hawks. This can disrupt the entire San Diego drug scene, so I'm going to push them to talk openly about the maps."

"I like it Paul, I hope it plays out that way. Now that we know they have someone following us, what do you think we should do? Should we end the trip and come back to San Diego?"

"Hmmm. I don't know if that's a good idea. They know where you and Penny both live, so unless you have another place to go that they don't know about and can't find, you're probably better off out there than you are coming back. I think you should just be careful, have fun, and let us try to cut this thing off back here. If we can shut down the top guys, the ones chasing after you have no reason to continue."

"That's what we were thinking, too."

"Ok, I'll keep in touch to let you know what's happening. What will you and Penny do?"

"Continue our ride. And we are going to get married somewhere along the way."

"Do you know where, yet? Or are you going to keep it a secret?"

"Maybe we do, but we're not sure yet. I'll let you know when we've figured it out. Right now though, we're taking our time and having a nice, leisurely lunch."

"Where are you now?" Asked the impatient voice over the noisy cell phone connection.

"We've been through every broken down, dusty, half-abandoned little burg on the road between Needles and Flagstaff on 'not-so-romantic' old Route 66 'til hell-won't-have-it-anymore. We're about to pull into Flagstaff for a good meal, a good bed, and no more of this bullshit chase, Arnie." Ferdy said with sarcasm he didn't try to control.

"See anything?"

"What the fuck are we supposed to see? Some people riding motorcycles painted up in the Stars and Stripes, with matching helmets and signs sewn on their backs saying, 'Easy Rider'?"

"Cut the shit, I don't need it. We finally got a name for the owner of the place on Caminito Castillo. He's Jim Schmidt. We found out by talking to the neighbors that he's a biker. We've had a guy sitting on the place for two days now, and he hasn't seen anyone. So, we had Jerry crack a door for a look around. No one there. And guess what?"

Sighing, Ferdy said, "What?"

"Her Mustang is in the garage. She's been with him—Schmidt."

"Okay, so the two of them are traveling together, stopped in Needles, and that's the last we know?" Ferdy asked.

"We know a little more. She's a biker, too. Mack gave that up to us when we leaned on him before they put him in jail. It didn't mean nothin' to us until we found out about Schmidt. Then when we hit her place yesterday to get the notebook, we looked in her garage and, bingo, no Mustang and no bike. Just a bunch of Harley Davidson manuals and biker stuff. We're guessing they left Needles on bikes they hauled over there in a truck. And we think she forgot her cell phone and left it in the truck or somewhere in the rental place. That's why the tracker got stuck on the van and truck rental joint."

"So, now what?"

"You're looking for a man and woman riding bikes along the 'Easy Rider' route."

"Feels like what we've been doing. It's a needle in a haystack: two motorcycles in maybe fifteen hundred miles of open road between California and the Louisiana State line."

"We're sending out more teams. You've got California, Arizona, and New Mexico. Another team has Oklahoma and Texas, and another has Arkansas and Louisiana."

"That's still a needle in a haystack; make that three haystacks."

"Look, you don't have to screw around with California since you're already in Flagstaff. You've only got Arizona and New Mexico to cover."

"Somehow, that doesn't make me feel any better, Arnie. But why do we care, now that we have the maps?"

"She might have copies, so we've still got to find her. Get your asses in gear. Tell Tommy to drive fast and not loaf along like he usually does. And ask a lot of questions; you know, like cops."

"We're gonna average about three miles an hour doin' that. There's gotta be a better way."

"I hope you find it, then. Carlos is ready to kill something."

"Okay, Arnie, tell Carlos to relax. Have a nice day." *Asshole . . . .*

Nineteen – Too Late

"Look, Jim! There's a wedding planner here in Farmington who can arrange a traditional Hopi or Navajo wedding. She can provide a shaman, or preacher, or justice of the peace, or whatever's needed. It says the marriage will be recognized in all U.S. states. And she'll arrange the marriage licenses, celebrations, accommodations, and anything else needed," Penny said with a big grin as she looked at the search results on her new phone.

They were sitting in the quiet lounge of the restaurant where they'd finished lunch and were spending an hour or two, relaxing over cocktails and deciding their next moves—and where to get married.

"Great! Call her!"

After a fifteen-minute phone call with much waiting while the woman checked her schedules and the information she had on people who could perform a traditional Native American wedding, Penny held her finger over the phone's microphone and said, "She said she can do it, but not for several days. Mid-next week would be the earliest. What do you think? I want to do it, don't you?"

"Can she arrange for it to be in the Great Kiva in Aztec?"

Penny relayed the question to the planner. "She says yes, but it has to be after four p.m. when there are no more tourists."

"That's perfect. We don't want any tourists around, anyway. Tell her yes!"

"Jim, this is too much fun! I want to celebrate, let's go out for a good dinner."

"Let's find a motel first and then go out. I need to get this road dirt out of my hair and off my face."

"Me too. Maybe there'll be a nice pool and spa."

Penny and Jim settled into a cozy booth by the fireplace in the Farmington Rustic Ranch Restaurant.

"Call them. I want to make sure they can get here," Penny said to Jim.

Jim found Steve in the few numbers he'd remembered and had added to his new phone's contacts list. He punched "call."

"Steve, It's Jim. I wanted to call to let you and Ali know about our wedding."

"Hey, man! Are you really going to do it?"

"Yes. Next Wednesday at four in the Great Kiva in the ruins in Aztec, New Mexico. Will you and Ali come?"

"Hell yes! If we get wheels up by seven, we can land in Farmington before noon. We'll get a car and meet you wherever you want. I can't wait to tell Alice."

"Great! This will be very casual, so you don't need to pack any dressy stuff. We don't have anything other than our riding leathers but jeans and casual shirts. We'll meet you at the airport at noon and help you get organized and then go somewhere to hang out until the wedding."

"Okay, that's the plan then. What have you heard from Daggett and the SDPD? Are they getting anywhere?"

"There's a lot to tell you about."

Jim went over the new ideas he and Penny had discovered, and the conversation with Daggett.

"I haven't heard yet about getting the notebook from Penny's place. I'm going to call to see what's new as soon as we finish."

"Then we should end this call so you can do that now, Jim. Things could be breaking minute by minute on that."

"I know. I just wanted to update you and Ali first. We'll talk later."

"Too late to call Morton. It's eight p.m. now—seven San Diego time, and he's probably at home for the evening."

"Try Daggett," Penny offered.

"He may not be up to date. They'll be holding back from anyone not in the department. Information is power, kinda thing . . . . But I'll try."

Before he could punch in Daggett's number, Jim's phone rang.

"Jim, it's Dale Morton."

"Hey, Dale. I was just thinking about trying to call you. What's the news?"

"Not good. Penny's place was hit before we got there. There's no notebook like the one Penny described. We combed the place looking for it, but it looks like someone found it first. The place had been searched—not ransacked—but clearly searched. They must have found it."

Jim had put his cell phone on speaker as soon as he realized it was Morton calling so Penny could listen in.

"Shit! Shit, shit, shit!" Penny yelled. "Are you still there? Go into my office and to my computer. It's set up as a video recorder with six cameras placed around my house. You should be able to see the thugs who did this. Maybe you'll be able to identify them."

"Your computer is trashed, Penny. They smashed the case, pulled the hard drive and must have taken it with them."

"The bastards! Okay then, go to Jim's house. I set his computer up to do remote viewing and recording. I checked to make sure it was all working before we left. You should be able to see everything up to the point they trashed my home computer."

"Jesus, Penny, that's genius!" Morton almost yelled.

Penny gave him the user ID, password, and the recorder app name and location.

"Okay, I'll get our best video forensics detective and our locksmith and go over there right away. It'll probably be tomorrow before I get back to you, though. I hope there's enough recorded that we can get an ID on at least one."

"Don't we all . . . ." Jim muttered. "Good luck. Call me if you need any information about the house." He added Morton's number to his contact list.

"I'm depressed. Let's go back to the motel and try to forget this, hon," Jim said to Penny.

Riding the few miles back to their motel room on Jim's bike, Penny held Jim tightly, pressing her head sideways against the back of his shoulder and squeezing his waist the entire distance.

"You were holding on pretty hard, are you okay?"

"Not really. Seems like everything is turning to shit right now— except for us. Let's get in bed and hold onto each other. I need to feel safe."

"Morton's right, you know. You are a genius . . . and cool . . . and sexy. Where have you been all my life?"

"Looking for love—in all the wrong places, I guess."

"Not anymore."

Twenty - Day Tripper

"What do you want to do for the next four days?" Jim asked Penny as they ate a leisurely breakfast. "Go on to eastern New Mexico and Taos and Santa Fe where they filmed the next scenes? That's where they shot the parade and jail scenes, and Nicolson joined the trip. We could do that as a round trip and be back here Tuesday afternoon or evening in plenty of time for our wedding."

"I don't want to do four days of hard riding, if that's what it'll take. We've been on the road, including the van drive, for four days now and I'd like to take it easy in whatever riding we do from here."

"Yeah, I can understand that. Here's an alternative: We could take short day trips out of here. No rides longer than a couple of hours with plenty of off-seat time, seeing things."

"That sounds good. What do you have in mind?"

"One could be a day trip to Durango. It's a cool small city with little shops you'd like: art stores, good restaurants, and bars. It's only around an hour from here."

"I like that."

"Another option is that, plus another hour's ride up to Silverton."

"What's in Silverton?"

"It's not as interesting as Durango, but the drive is spectacular. Great mountain scenery and fun roads—if the tourist traffic isn't too bad."

"Sounds like you've done this before."

"I have. I used to ski at Purgatory, just outside of Durango, now and then. But I also rode this entire area after Annie died."

"A trip of remembrance?"

"More like a trip of trying to run away from memories."

"I'm sorry, Jim. It seems like it always keeps coming back to Annie . . . ."

"No, I'm the one who should be sorry. I could have told you about riding this area without bringing Annie into it."

"Will you ever forget?"

". . . Probably not. But that doesn't mean she controls my life. I don't think about her when I'm with you. And when I do think about her now, it's more like knowing I've reached a turning point in my life . . . going around a corner. Going around a corner, and there you are."

Softly, Penny said, "Okay, I like the idea of Durango and maybe Silverton. We can decide that while we're on the ride. What else?"

"Mesa Verde. Do you know about Mesa Verde?"

"Only that it's in the Four Corners region and is claimed to have some of the most complete and spectacular Anasazi ruins anywhere. Have you been there too?"

"Yes, and I want to show it to you. You won't believe the feelings you'll have when you see the cliff dwellings and the spectacular canyons there. I want to be with you when you first see it. If you've never seen those kinds of ruins before, you'll get a completely different perspective about the America you live in."

"What do you mean?"

"The Europeans didn't bring 'civilization' to an empty, primitive, beautiful land. There was a lot going on here before they arrived—and started fucking things up."

"Don't get me started on that. Is that an easy, one-day trip, too?"

"The riding's about the same. It's a loop trip. We take 170 north to 160 west and then follow a trail into the heart of the park. That's around an hour and fifteen minutes. After we see the park, we can return by looping west and south, and back here. So, the riding is under three hours, but the day will depend on how much hiking you want to do."

"I'm going to want to see everything."

"I thought so. That's one of the reasons I like you so much. You're interested in the same stuff I am."

"That's two days. We've got four. What else?"

"Another option is the Durango-Silverton ride with an extension to Ouray."

"Ouray? Never heard of it. What is it, another ruin?"

"No, it's a little town an hour past Silverton that you won't believe. It looks like someone helicoptered an entire, perfect, turn-of-the-century, New England village into a canyon between huge mountains. It was the biggest surprise of all my visits to Colorado."

"Then I think I want to see it. Do we add that to our Durango-Silverton trip?"

"Not exactly. We don't want to make it a full round-trip in one day. That won't leave enough time for sightseeing. We'll split the trip into two days and spend the night in some cute little hotel in Ouray, have dinner, and a wonderful evening."

"I like this. We still will have another day to fill, but do we have to do it riding? What about a day without motorcycles?"

"I think that's a good idea, and I think it should be your choice."

They extended their stay in the Courtyard hotel through the following Wednesday. Jim made reservations for Ali and Steve for the night before, and the night of the wedding, giving them options for their stay. They sat with their smart phones in the lobby bar, searching Google for a place to stay in Ouray. Forcing the events back in San Diego out of their minds, they relaxed and found their zeal for seat-time waning. A lazy, late-morning cocktail in the empty bar was the perfect thing. Given the news from Morton, they started to rationalize, hoping now that the thugs had the damn notebook, they'd be left alone and able to forget about Mack and his world.

"But somehow, it all seems naïve, Jim. Things like this just don't go away on their own. This has to be investigated, prosecuted, and people have to go to jail. And even then—"

"I know what you're saying, hon. But let's try to believe it, anyway."

"Don't you think you should call Morton and see what they've found on your computer? They should have been there by now."

"Hi Jim, we're still at your place. Is Penny listening? Bingo! We got two guys coming in the back door. They were wearing ball caps down low over their foreheads—but the camera Penny had on the floor—hidden in the planter nailed them both before they found the video equipment. We know them, and we know who they work for. Downtown is putting arrest warrants out for them now. We've got breaking and entering, destruction of property, theft, and everything we need to hold them while we trap the others. That remote recording setup was brilliant, Penny. And hiding that camera down low like that was even more brilliant. We should make you a cop!"

"Does this tie into Mack, Dale?" Penny asked.

"Don't know. It's too early to tell. But, that fight he was in when he nearly killed that guy was over something big. And this is big. But we have to find the people who hit Penny's and get that notebook. That's job number one right now."

"Okay, Dale. We'll let you get back to it. Thanks for the update and good luck."

"Thanks, you two. Take care of yourselves. This isn't over until it's over; you need to assume they're still looking for you."

"We know. Maybe we'll go hide in some ancient ruins until this blows over," Jim said, laughing.

"Do you want another cocktail; Jack on the rocks? Let's sit and talk a little more. I'm fine if we do nothing more today. This is a nice place."

"It's too early for a drink that strong. I think I want light Jack Daniels with soda and ice."

The waitress delivered the new drinks as the low sun was lighting the still empty cocktail lounge with a rich, golden glow. It was a pleasant way to end a day without the roar of the Harleys' exhaust notes, constant wind in their faces, and dust covering their riding suits and face shields.

"I think I've driven you to the point where you never want to hear anything of Annie again, and I don't blame you. But, I've been unfair, we've never talked about Bruce. You told me he was killed in that accident, but you haven't told me anything about him as a person, or your relationship with him other than that strange comment you made about *hurting* several days ago. I don't want to push you about things you may not want to talk about yet, but I want to give you the chance to tell me whenever you want to."

Staring at her drink, swirling the plastic mixing stick, Penny said, "Not sure I want to. I don't know how I feel about it yet, all these years later. It was a very mixed kind of relationship."

"Mixed?"

"Yes, love—alternating with hate."

"Hate, that's pretty strong."

"I can't call it anything else. It was the most—what do they call it in the tech world—binary relationship ever."

"Never heard anyone use that word in describing a man-woman relationship before. But I know what you mean: one minute it's love and the next minute, hate?"

"Okay, so now we are talking about it . . . . I loved him very much in the first years after we married. He'd been a college sweetheart, and we grew closer together as we went into our senior year. I think we both knew that after we graduated, we'd drift apart if we didn't do something. So, he took me out to a fancy downtown restaurant and proposed over dessert and champagne—which I knew was going to happen. There was nothing

152

subtle about it—and there was nothing subtle about Bruce. You always knew what he wanted long before he said it."

"Was he a jock? Most jocks are like that."

"He wasn't on any of the school teams, but he was always playing intramural sports. Whatever the sport of the season was, that's what he was playing. He lived the life of a jock without being a real jock. And, of course, that meant going out with the guys, watching every fucking sport on TV, and talking jock talk."

"Doesn't seem like your type. How did you get past that?"

"His charm. And warmth—and the fun. He was popular around campus."

"Chick magnet?"

"Yes, I guess. It seemed there was always competition to be his date, or be seen with him."

"I'm surprised, you seem so strong and self-assured; like you don't need anyone to validate yourself."

"That was then, and I was a different person. I didn't have any self-assurance in those days. I had good grades, a lot of girlfriends, but few boyfriends. But Bruce was a tough guy, and he pushed me to be tough just like him. After we married, he refused to take my side in disputes with friends or contractors. If I complained to him about being treated unfairly, or some slight, hoping he'd take my side and fix it, he'd say, 'It's your problem, don't look for me to be your daddy. You take care of it—and don't lose!' So that's why I'm who I am now."

"He was a real softy, then?" Jim said with a wry smile.

"Ha, yes, a real softy . . . . But I could have dealt with that—if it wasn't for the other things."

"The real things?"

"Yes, two things. The friction over them added up to the hating point. It wasn't continuous, by the way, but too frequently."

"Such as?"

"He never stopped being one of the boys. Going out without even asking me if I wanted to go along. Staying out, drinking after Padres or Chargers games, or after their all-important summertime, slow-pitch softball games. Coming back half drunk and belligerent if I asked any questions; on and on. That stuff and his Mission Bay Sports Club 'meetings'," using air quotes to emphasize the word *meetings*. "A group of guys that thought they were still in high school and acted about the same."

"What happened?"

"Fights. We'd fight, if you want to call it that. He'd do all the hitting, and I'd do all the hurting."

"He was abusing you? Why did you stay around?"

"I don't know. I guess I thought it was all about learning to live in a marriage and compromising."

"Sounds like you did all the compromising."

"I did—except for one thing . . . the other *thing*."

"What was the other *thing*?"

"Children; I refused to have children. And that was a big problem for him. He thought we should have kids like everyone else. But I did *not* want to bring kids into a marriage I had concerns about. He thought that threatened his manhood and such bullshit."

"Sounds horrible, fighting all the time . . . ."

"No, things would be okay for a while—until the next time. I mean it wasn't weekly or anything like that. It was more like a few times a year. Things would go well between us; we'd go riding with friends, or sometimes on weekend trips to fun places around Southern California. There were some nice guys and wives or girlfriends in the group, and it would all seem worth it—until the next blowup."

"So, is that how things were—at a standoff until . . . until the crash?"

"No, I walked out on him around a year before that happened. I decided I wasn't going to keep dealing with it."

"But why were you with him when the crash happened?"

"He kept after me to move back by trying to get me involved with our friends again, thinking having fun with them would make me come back. They were all going to Borrego Springs for a music weekend, which had always been one of our group's favorite things. So, we were riding in a group—a very loose grouping—spaced safely apart, not like a pack of bikes, you know? More like pairs of bikes spaced several car lengths apart. That's why I think the accident happened; the jerk didn't want to wait for us all to pass and tried to dart in between the pair in front of us and Bruce and me."

"You must have had very mixed—sorry, that's the word you used—feelings about it ending that way."

"I did. I was lost at times, and at other times I told myself it was my time to get a new start. After a few months I realized it wasn't because I'd lost a love I'd never be able to replace, but more just the feeling of being alone again. Finally, I started dealing with it: putting on my mental armor every morning—Bruce taught me that—along with my make-up and favorite clothes, and going out into the world and throwing myself into my job."

"How long ago was this?"

"The crash was a little over four years ago."

Jim took Penny's hand, nodding his head. They sat together in silence as the sun settled below the horizon and the mood lights in the lounge came on. People started drifting into the bar.

Twenty-One - Closing In

"Why are we still doing this if they have the fuckin' notebook, Tommy?"

"They want to find out who she talked to about it—and whether she made any copies and gave them to someone," Tommy answered.

"Look at this map; nothing but desert. What are we supposed to do, drive up 160 to 163 and go through Monument Valley, then back to 160 and over to Farmington on 164. That's supposed to be the 'Easy Rider' route. There's nothing out there except the park and a bunch of little Indian villages along the way."

"Good. Two bikers—especially if one's a girl—should be noticeable out there, Ferdy."

"Still feels like we're gonna be looking for Captain America on his Stars 'n' Stripes chopper. Call Arnie to see if he has anything new."

Tommy dialed his cell phone.

"Hey Arnie, Tommy here. We're about to head out to Monument Valley and then over to Farmington. Anything new on your end?"

"Only that we had a local Needles guy go to that van and truck rental place to see Fred again."

"Do you mean Vince? Jesus Christ, I hear he's an animal."

"Yeah, Vince. He got a little out of him. What you're doing sounds like the right thing. We think they were going on the same route you're planning to take. Get going and keep your eyes open. Ask questions, but be cool about it. You don't want to raise any suspicions."

"I'm a little afraid to ask this, Arnie, because I'm not sure I want to know the answer; but what happened with the van and truck guy?"

"He's in the river."

"Oh shit, did he have to do that?"

"Come on, you know about Vince. You shouldn't be surprised."

"Yeah, I know about Vince. Why they keep him around is beyond me."

"He gets the job done. Simple."

"Yeah, and then some. Talk to you later." Tommy dropped the cell phone in the center console. "He said he's in the river, Ferdy."

"Christ, this keeps getting deeper and deeper."

"I loved our trip to Ouray, Jim. Nice highways with beautiful mountain scenery. I'm glad you thought of it, and these day trips."

They were back in the Farmington Courtyard's lounge after finishing their return ride from Ouray, Silverton, and Durango.

"Yeah, and how did you like that little hotel? I haven't slept in anything smaller than a queen-sized bed in years, but I kind of liked being cozied up to you under a mountain of blankets. Sure gets cold up there at night though."

"But I loved it. I sleep better when it's cold like that," Penny said.

"Yes, you *did* sleep well, didn't you?" Jim said, emphasizing *did*.

"I have to get a good night's sleep now and then. I can be ready for the next night that way. Isn't that a good trade-off?"

"Would that be tonight?"

"You'll see. So, tomorrow we do Mesa Verde and lots of ruins?"

"Yes. We need to leave early to get on the first tours so we don't have to wait around behind a bunch of tourists. Quick breakfast at six-thirty and on the road by seven-thirty?"

"I can do it. Traveling with you like this, I can do whatever is needed."

"Great. By the way, we haven't heard from Morton in two days. I think I should call the detective to see if there's news."

Jim hit the call symbol on Morton's box in the contacts list and activated the speaker.

"Hi Dale. We've been on a two-day ride up through the Rockies and may have been out of cell phone range. Anything new?"

"Yes, a few things. The two guys who hit Penny's place work for a drug dealer named Carlos Garcia. He's the guy Mack beat up in the big fight. Our drug guys think the fight was over the notebook. The theory is that Carlos found out that Mack was compiling it, and either felt threatened by it, or wanted it for his own purposes. Word on the street is that Mack owes Carlos a lot of money from deals and had been ducking him. Could be the notebook was a bargaining chip in the debt debate, but we don't know. This may be the break our drug guys have been waiting for to roll Mack on Carlos's drug operation."

"So, have you picked up the two guys yet, or are you holding off?"

"We've been tailing them to find out who their connections are before we lock them up. We don't want to play our hand too soon. But I think we have what we want from them now and the plan is to grab them tomorrow morning. We want to work them a little before word gets out that we have them for this caper."

"Glad to hear this, Dale. Penny and I can breathe easier now and enjoy our trip a lot more when you have those guys. I'm hoping they'll back off when they know their jig's up."

"Yes, but you've still got to be careful. These people aren't rational like the rest of us."

"You're telling me! We're going on a day ride tomorrow to Mesa Verde and may be out of touch again. But we'll call when we get back at the end of the afternoon. Thanks for taking my calls."

"No problem, I understand what you're going through. Take care of yourselves."

Jim turned off his phone. "Penny, honey, I'm bushed. Let's go to the room and call room service. I want to eat in bed and not move again today."

"You have the best ideas!"

"Hi guys, what can I get you?" The bartender behind the Courtyard's long, polished counter asked the two men who'd just slid onto barstools.

"I'll have a Coors draft, if you have it," Tommy said.

"Me too," added Ferdy.

"Comin' up."

Placing bar napkins down before he sat the tall mugs of beer in front of the two, the bartender said, "Aren't you one night early?"

"Early? Why do you ask that?"

"The monthly Rotary get-together is tomorrow night. Aren't you Rotarians?"

"No, we're medical supplies salesmen. Why would you think we're Rotarians?"

"How you dress. Short-sleeve business shirts, ties, no jackets, khaki pants, and tassel loafers: Rotary uniforms."

"Ha, ha. No, sorry, just dressing the way that's comfortable out here in the desert and still looks businesslike."

"Yeah, I guess so. Believe me, that's how all the downtown business men dress around here."

"Well, sorta makes sense doesn't it: business dress is business dress. By the way, maybe you can answer a question for me?"

"Yeah, what is it? Bartenders know all . . . ."

"Do you get many bikers through here following the old 'Easy Rider' route? I hear it's a big thing these days."

"Yeah, depending on the time of year naturally. This supposedly was right on the film crew's route as they went from Monument Valley to Taos. There weren't any movie shots made around here, but the story is they came through. Why?"

"Just curious. Have there been any through here in the last day or so, or even today? I'd love to talk to some of them just to find out what it's like. You know, why are they doin' it? What are they lookin' for, how does it feel, that kind of shit?"

"There's a couple staying here right now that have been following the route. But, I guess they decided to take a couple of days off to see the sights around here. They just came back from someplace an hour or so ago.

I heard them talking about Mesa Verde tomorrow. Maybe you can catch them in the breakfast bar in the morning."

"Mesa what?"

"Mesa Verde. V-E-R-D-E."

"What is it?"

"It's a world-famous cluster of cliff dwellings an hour or two northwest of here."

"So, it's a day trip kind of thing?"

"Yeah. Lots of tourists stay here to go up there. Some of them go back, day after day, to see it all. There's a nice driving loop most people take: 160 into the park from the east, and then 160 out to the west, then 491 south."

"What are the roads like going up there?"

"Remote. Nothing out there but a few scattered little houses. No towns, no services, nothing."

Tommy looked sideways at his partner with scheming eyes. "Okay, we might check it out. Sounds like something we shouldn't miss now that we're here."

"That's true. It's a world wonder."

"We need a room. Do you know if there are vacancies?"

"Last I knew, there were. This is still the off-season: there's snow in the higher elevations that keeps some folks away until spring break."

"See, the clothes worked. We didn't even need the bolo ties, shithead!"

"Fuck you, Tommy."

"Okay, okay, easy, Ferdy, I was just kidding! Tomorrow morning we're gonna hang out in the breakfast bar area and look for two people dressed like bikers from the time it opens until we see them. We'll try to listen in on their conversation to see if they talk about how they're going."

"Then what?" Ferdy asked.

"We'll follow them at a safe distance, trying to look like tourists, and look for a spot to trap them on the way out."

"Yeah, yeah, yeah, that's obvious. What are we going to do when we have that decided?"

"Wait for them. Force them off the road. You're gonna be holding the shotgun on them, Ferdy, old friend. We tie them up, load them into the back seat and take them someplace where they'll talk to us. Get them to tell us everything about the notebook and who knows about it."

"Sounds like an all-day job; we're gonna need lunches. Are we going to pound on them?"

"Look, you've been doin' this long enough to know we do whatever we've gotta do. It would be nice if we could just threaten them and they caved, but that probably won't happen. I hope we don't have to do anything more than slap one of them around a little, but we have to be ready to do whatever it takes. We've got knuckles, knives and rope; something will work."

"Then what?"

"I don't know, I don't want another murder on my sheet. We shouldn't off people unless we're the ones who are threatened. If we can get it out of them without doing anything too heavy, we might be able to let them go. If we ever get caught, a little assault isn't going to add much to my sheet, and I could live with that."

"You gettin' soft?"

"Ferdy, I'm getting tired . . . tired of knockin' people around. This business is getting a little old for me. I hope this will be easy—for them and us," Tommy said.

"Let's go buy sandwiches for tomorrow."

Twenty-Two - Mesa Verde

"The Anasazi peoples—Hopi and Pueblos—who built these buildings, populated this mesa and these canyons for over one thousand years before they were driven out by droughts and bad crops," the guide told the group as they hiked a rising trail to a series of wooden ladders propped against the cliff face.

"And in Canyon de Chelly, south of here, the U.S. Army, led by Kit Carson, drove them from their homes and force-marched them hundreds of miles to the east to their new homeland," The guide continued, frowning as he spoke the words "new homeland."

Penny and Jim climbed one ladder taking them to a ledge wide enough for a few people to stand on, and then climbed the next ladder, leading to a higher ledge and another ladder, which led to a final broad ledge that was the main floor level of the cliff dwellings. The climb, while not dangerous for anyone in decent condition, was a challenge for people with acrophobia as the view down while climbing the ladders was exaggerated by the drop-off to the dry river beds far below. The combined effect discouraged many would-be cliff dwelling tourists. Penny climbed the series of ladders without a second thought, never looking down.

"I thought Kit Carson was one of the good guys," Penny said as she started up a ladder. "At least that's the impression I had from my high school history classes."

"Yeah, well history books have to be approved by people appointed by politicians. You can't always believe what you're taught in high school."

"Or church," Penny responded. "I decided that when I found out that the Roman Emperor Constantine appointed the council who decided what went into the Bible. What do you suppose his objectives were?"

"You can only imagine. Hey, I see you know the secret to climbing challenging trails and mountain paths."

"Do you mean never looking down?"

"Yes. How did you get comfortable doing it?"

"By knowing I'd scare the shit out of myself if I looked down. I used my fear to conquer my fear."

"Could you look down now?"

"Maybe, but I wouldn't like it. If it's too high, I always feel like I'm going to wet my pants!"

"How do you expect to go back down? You have to look down to see the next rung in the ladder."

"By only looking at the next rung."

"That's how I do it, too!"

"You bastard. You had me thinking you were the great mountaineer, afraid of nothing."

"I'm from Indiana, remember. The highest thing I ever experienced was standing on a milking stool."

They spent the day on various tours and hikes, gaining an appreciation for the living and organizational skills that existed before the Europeans arrived and brought their skills and technology—and violence and diseases. They marveled that, while the first of the Anasazi cultures had disappeared well before the Europeans arrived, they left outstanding examples of their level of sophistication dating back a thousand years. Penny and Jim stood looking in awe at their accomplishments. Jim started into a narrative of how the European diseases decimated the native Americans—hundreds of years before the brutal Indian wars—and how it is a highly suppressed story, not fitting into the modern narrative of American Exceptionalism that politicians love to talk about.

"Please don't talk about it, Jim," Penny asked. "I'm having a beautiful day and I don't want it ruined with the truth about governments."

Well behind Penny and Jim, but in the same guided tour group

"Enough of this crap, Tommy. I'm tired of following them around these dusty trails and I can't look at another old mud brick and stone building. What's so important about a bunch of Indians who lived here a thousand years ago. So they had brick buildings before some other places did; big deal. Look what it got them, in the big picture, they're still living in mud brick buildings," Ferdy complained.

"Asshole, try to get some perspective of history. Think of what it was like, living out here in a desert with no running water, electricity, cell phones, or TV. No doctors, no medicines, livin' off corn and squash, and they did all this!" Tommy replied.

"Yeah, so they made pretty baskets. BFD!"

"Okay, I can see you've absorbed all the culture you can for your lifetime, but I'm tired of this, too. We heard them say they're gonna take 160 out to the west so they don't have to go back the same way. Let's go find a place to set up our ambush."

After hours of guided tours, walking several miles in the hot sun, and climbing countless wooden ladders in and out of adobe buildings, Penny said, "I'm exhausted, Jim. This has been wonderful, but I'm 'ruined' out," air quoting the word *ruined.*

"Me too. I'm ready to ride back and sit in the bar by the fireplace again with a good drink and nothing but dinner in mind. Not thinking about thugs in San Diego has been a refreshing change."

"I wasn't going to bring it up."

"Thanks for that, I don't know why I did. But, now and then it pops back up in my mind and I can't push it back. Lead the way, hon!"

With the parking lots almost empty and all but a few straggling tourists gone, they started their Harleys and headed out the dirt road toward the highway. They followed 160 west and then 491 south, hoping to return to the Courtyard before sundown. At a sign announcing "Shiprock 10 MILES", where they would turn onto 64 for the final leg back to Farmington, with Jim leading and Penny following ten feet off his left rear—the road curved around a clump of large rocks on the opposite side of the road. As they rode past, Jim noticed a white SUV around the backside of the rock pile, circling behind it, and heading for the highway behind them. It pulled onto the road one hundred yards behind them. Jim was immediately suspicious and watched it in his rear-view mirror. He reached under his seat into the compartment where the .45 hid. As the SUV accelerated and gained ground on them, Jim noticed the passenger side widow had lowered, and a long, black gun barrel appeared.

"Penny, do you hear me?" Jim said into his helmet-to-helmet radio.

"I hear you. Did you see the white car that came out from those rocks?"

"It's trouble. It looks like there's a gun sticking out of the passenger window. They may try to pass us and block the road."

"What do we do?"

"When I say, 'hit your brakes,' hit them as hard as you can without sliding. I'll wait a few seconds so we don't crash into each other, and then do the same. They should fly by and that'll give us a chance to turn and head back the other way. We'll go off-road at a dirt trail I saw back there before the rockpile. I'll pass you, and you follow me. They won't be able to keep up."

"Okay. Just tell me when."

The SUV pulled into the on-coming traffic lane, obviously getting in position to pull alongside or pass them. *I'm not going to screw around with these guys; I've seen enough of their handiwork.* Jim slid the .45 out of its compartment, then momentarily taking both hands off the bars, loaded a shell into the firing chamber, doing it quickly in his lap so the move wouldn't be seen from behind. He set the safety to the 'off' position. As the Navigator pulled even with Penny, Jim yelled, "now" into his helmet microphone. Penny hit both front and rear brakes at the same time and was well behind the SUV within seconds. Jim applied his brakes after seeing that Penny now had enough clearance to start her one-eighty turn. But as the SUV pulled even with him, the driver matched Jim's braking and bulled across the center line into Jim's lane as the passenger leveled the shotgun at Jim's chest and signaled a pull-up motion. He yelled something undistinguishable. Jim rotated his left arm straight out, pointing the .45 at the shotgunner, mouthing, "Fuck you!" The passenger mouthed the same thing back and pointed the short-barreled pump-gun at Jim's head. Jim's split-second response was to pull the trigger at near point-blank range, hitting the man full in the forehead. A momentary look of surprise spread over his face as he fell back into the SUV, the shotgun dropping from his hands and bouncing off the car's window sill.

The shotgun, falling and pointed at Jim's leg and the Harley's engine, fired from the impact with the windowsill. It hit both. The shot pattern sent most of the pellets into the V-Twin's rear cylinder, but the outer fringe of the pattern tore into Jim's knee. Most of the buckshot load hit the top of the engine cylinder in the valve train area, causing the engine to freeze and sending the bike into a severe skid that threw Jim over the handlebars and into the ditch alongside the road. The Harley cartwheeled down the road another fifty feet before landing on its side, badly bent and smoking. Penny, watching over her shoulder, had seen this happening as she started her U-turn and quickly completed a full three-sixty, heading for Jim, lying motionless in the ditch near a small rock pile.

Jim was conscious when Penny arrived, but dizzy and unaware of the situation.

"Jim, are you all right? Jesus, look at the blood. You're bleeding from the back of your knee, honey. The shot must have hit you there."

Pulling away the tattered fragments of his jeans, she looked at Jim's knee, "Oh my God, it must have hit the artery in the back of your knee; it's pulsing blood."

Jim, now more awake and frightened by the sound of fear in Penny's voice, leaned over to look for himself. "Yeah, that's pretty bad. I'll pull my belt off to use as a tourniquet. Help me with it."

They ripped the belt out of the belt loops and wound it around Jim's thigh, slightly above his knee. First Penny, and then Jim, twisted and tightened it with all their strength so the blood pulsing slowed, but did not completely stop.

"This isn't good enough, Jim. We need a real tourniquet and someone stronger than me to tighten it."

"It'll have to do for now. What is that car doing? Have they gone on, or are they coming back?"

Penny crouched up just enough so she could see over the rock pile. "The car is sitting there, off to the side of the road. It looks like the driver is leaning over to the passenger side, checking on him. Did you hit him when you shot?"

"Oh yes. Right in the forehead. He's probably trying to see if he's dead. Look, he'll be coming back for us in a rage, we've got to protect ourselves. Do you see my gun?"

Penny scanned around the immediate area in a three-sixty circle, "No, I don't see it. The shotgun is laying out by the road though. Should I get it?"

"Yes, go get it before the driver comes back this way. We'll need it."

Penny crawled out to the edge of the road, grabbed the gun and brought it back to the rock pile.

"Look to see if there are more shells in the magazine. You know how to do that with a pump-gun?"

"Hell, yes. My dad taught me all about shooting these things when I was in high school." She unscrewed the end stop, looked into the magazine and found it was full, except for the one shot that had been fired.

"Penny, I'm getting faint. You're going to . . . to have to . . . to handle things. Can you shoot it if you need to?"

"Yes."

"Can you shoot a man—if you need to?"

"If it comes down to him or us, I can shoot him."

"Okay, pump a new shell into the chamber and hide behind these rocks and watch what he does. I'll use my cell phone to call 911."

Shivering from nervousness, she said, "Okay, honey. Oh God, Jim, please get someone here fast!"

As Jim called for emergency assistance and waited to speak to someone, he noted the roadside sign giving the ten-mile distance to Shiprock. It seemed like a long way with blood pumping out of his knee at an alarming rate. But at least he could direct the emergency team to their position.

"He's coming!" Penny yelled.

The Navigator had turned around and was now creeping back toward them, using the smoking motorcycle lying by the road as its target. It stopped by the Harley, fifty feet up the road from their hiding place. But it wasn't a hiding place; the rock pile would give Jim and Penny only a scant amount of protection.

The driver remained in the Navigator, thinking he'd try to sweet-talk her. "Show yourselves. I don't want to hurt you, I just want to ask for some information."

Fat chance! "Then why the hell was your guy pointing that shotgun at us?" Penny yelled back.

"Just getting your attention. But we weren't going to shoot anyone."

"Sounds like bullshit." She yelled back. "Just leave us alone so we can get medical help as fast as possible. We don't have anything for you. Who are you anyway? And why would you think we have something you want?"

"Mack told us you would."

"Oh, fuck Mack! What did he tell you I have?"

"A notebook. A notebook of maps and codes."

"Well, if I had it I sure as hell wouldn't have it out here. I'm on vacation, for God's sake!"

"We have the notebook now. I want to know if you told anyone about it, or made copies and gave them to anyone."

"We have it? Who is 'we?'"

"Don't worry about that. Tell me what you did with the book when you had it."

"Nothing. I don't even know what it is. It didn't concern me, so I put it away."

"How do I know that you're not lying?"

"Why would I lie? I don't care about something I don't know anything about."

"Look, I'll give you a good deal. Get your friend in my car and I'll take you to get medical help."

It was an obvious trap. Penny knew he didn't care about Jim, it was only a way to get her in the car. *Then what?*

"I've just told you everything. You've got it now, so leave us alone."

"I'm coming to you. I'll leave my gun here and we can just talk this over."

"Don't! Don't get out of your car."

"Listen, little honey, I've dealt with a lot of bad characters in my time and you're not intimidating me. We can settle this peacefully."

"Don't get out of your car."

"Are you threatening me? You don't know who you're messing with." He opened the door.

Penny hadn't been showing the shotgun. Now she raised it from beside her leg and slid it to the top of the rock pile.

"Please, just stay in your car."

Tommy did a SWAT-cop maneuver and rolled out of the car, coming up on one knee, leveling his handgun at Penny, saying, "I'm not interested in killing you, but if I have to shoot you, I will. You killed my partner and I'm losing patience with this."

Penny wasn't about to lose any more time getting help for Jim. "This shotgun is unlocked and has a full magazine. Don't make me pull the trigger. I have a wounded friend and I'm not going to fuck around with you."

"I don't think you'll do it."

Penny fired a shot at the open car door that blew an eight-inch hole in the sheet metal and pasted the door back against the doorframe. "I think I would."

Startled, Tommy decided he'd better end things as soon as possible. No chick could stare down a bull rush, so he charged at Penny using the combat technique of zig-zagging back and forth, avoiding the open ground in front of the rock pile. It could have been a suicidal move, but one he thought would intimidate her and affect her aim—or even that she'd panic, bail out, and duck behind the rockpile. In his experience, women usually chickened out in similar situations.

"You must be crazy," Penny yelled as she tracked him with the gun barrel. As he crossed in front of the Navigator, she fired but the shot passed behind Tommy, blowing the entire windshield into the back seat in tiny fragments. Startled by the sound of a full twelve gauge shot load hissing and screaming only inches past his ear, Tommy stumbled and ducked to the ground in a defensive posture, lying on his side, trying to steady his handgun in a firing position. Penny stayed with him, maintaining her aim as he tried to rise to a shooting stance. She flicked the reload pump, charging the firing chamber with a new round, and in nearly the same motion, pulled the trigger. The twelve-gauge's full shot pattern hit Tommy in his lower abdominal area and doubled him over, felling him face down in the dirt and gravel. A huge puddle of blood quickly formed under his body. He bled out in a matter of minutes, or even seconds.

"Penny, what's happening? Are you okay?" Jim said with a weak voice.

"I shot him and I think he's dead, or dying fast. How are you doing with an emergency crew?"

"They're on their way, but they wanted to know if there's an active shooter situation going on. I told them there was, and they'd need a police escort."

"Call them back and tell them it's over and they won't have to worry about that. Tell them we need them to concentrate on getting you to a hospital."

"I will, but I'm sure they're going to be cautious and not let the paramedics come to me until they've checked it out for themselves," Jim said in a dry, ragged, weak voice.

"Jesus, they could spend hours doing that. Tell them the assailants are dead and they need to get you help fast!"

She crawled over to where Jim was lying in his own puddle of blood, hanging onto his cell phone.

"I'm sorry, honey, I'm so sorry. It's my fault." She kneeled to hold his head in her lap, repeatedly kissing his forehead.

"Tighten up that tourniquet as much as you can. I need every drop we can save. It's a long way to Shiprock," Jim said as he faded.

Penny lost it as she sat with Jim's head in her lap, crying and praying to hear the wail of sirens in the distance. *Where the hell are they?*

Jim slipped his hand over hers to let her know he was still there, hanging on, "I love you, Penny Lane," he whispered.

"Oh Jesus, Jim, please stay with me. Please."

After what seemed to be hours, but was only a few minutes, sirens sounded in the distance. *Please, please, please hurry. He doesn't seem to be breathing . . . .*

Damn, they're stopping way back there by the Navigator. "Over here! We're over here!" she shouted.

They're looking at the dead bodies and scouting around like they think there are more people with guns. We told them that's all over. Fuck!

"There aren't any more of them, it's safe," Penny screamed, "You've got to get my friend to a hospital!"

"Who are you, lady?" a deputy asked.

"I'm with the person who called you. He's my fiancé. He's bleeding badly and is going to die if you don't get him to a hospital. They shot him."

"What happened here? Who shot these people?"

"I can tell you all about that later. Can't we just load him in the ambulance and go?"

"Get the ambulance up here and have them check the guy out," the deputy said to his partner.

"Okay." He spoke something into his shoulder radio and waved at the ambulance.

"This guy has lost a lot of blood, there's almost no pulse," the EMT said to his driver.

"Let's get him loaded and on an IV."

They strapped Jim onto a gurney and pushed it into the wagon. Penny followed and insisted on riding in the back.

"Sit over there, 'mam, try to keep him awake," the EMT said as he applied and tightened a real tourniquet.

Awake? His eyes are closed, he's hardly breathing, and he's turning grey-white. "Where is the nearest hospital? Can they give him blood?" Penny asked the technician.

"It's in Shiprock. It's a small hospital, but they have an ER and Urgent Care."

"I don't think Urgent Care is going to cut it," Penny said.

"No kidding!"

"Please, stop," Penny said with irritation.

"Sorry, 'mam. Just trying to make sure you understand what kind of shape he's in."

"My name is Penny."

Penny rubbed Jim's hands and said meaningless, hopeful things as the technician inserted the IV and started a bag of saline. The driver advised them to fasten their seatbelts since it was going to be a fast, rough ride. One patrol car led, sirens blasting, warning the non-existent traffic. The second patrol car stayed behind, the deputies documenting the crime scene.

The driver called Shiprock to advise the ER of their situation. "We're bringing in a patient who needs blood yesterday. We don't know what blood type because he's not carrying an ID with medical information."

A voice on the radio came back, saying, "We're out of O-neg right now. We've been trying to get it out here, but don't have an answer on when, yet. We'll have to blood type him."

"I don't think he'll make it if we have to wait thirty minutes to do that."

Penny, who'd been listening to the radio conversation, yelled to the driver, "I'm O negative. Can't we use my blood?"

"Are you sure? How do you know?"

"I had a bad motorcycle accident a few years ago and had to have blood. You don't forget your blood type after something like that. But I even have a medical slip in my wallet saying O-neg."

"Companion says she's O-neg and wants to use her blood. Says she's carrying a medical card that states her blood type. What do you think?" the driver asked the hospital. "Can we do a side by side, indirect transfusion?"

"Maybe, but we need to get her history. How far out are you?" The hospital answered.

"Five minutes."

"Okay, we'll have a team meet you at the door."

"Lady—" the technician started to say.

"My name is Penny. I've got clean blood; I've never used drugs other than a joint now and then, I don't have hepatitis, and I don't have any STDs. They can call my clinic in San Diego to get my records; I had my annual blood tests six months ago," Penny said.

"Sounds good. That's what I was going to ask you. They'll do tests anyway to double check types and look for antibodies and other things. But they'll probably decide to get the transfusion started first and then they can test for those issues while we're transfusing. They can deal with any complications later. But we've got to get him there alive, first."

Twenty-Three - Shiprock

April 25th 2013

"Jim, can you hear me? Are you awake? Please say something if you can," Penny pleaded to the still figure in the adjacent bed.

He'd been in a coma-like silence with only occasional spasms or nearly inaudible coughing sounds while the transfusion was in process. His heart rate and blood pressure had been below danger levels, but some color had returned to his death-grey face in the past few minutes. The last coughing spell had seemed a little stronger and his chest had heaved a little harder. Were these the good signs of a recovering patient, or insignificant distinctions without a difference—or worse?

"Jim, honey, can you hear me?" Penny's voice trembled with fear and sobs she tried to hold back, but couldn't.

Jim's little emergency room: two beds and two chairs, a wall of equipment surrounded on three sides by privacy curtains drawn out on ceiling-mounted tracks, provided a minimum of seclusion. The outer room was midnight silent except for the sounds of staff scurrying by outside the small gathering of Jim, Penny, the ER doctor, and nurse.

Faintly, a hoarse sound came from Jim's unmoving mouth, "I'm coming, Penny. I'm coming back. He . . . he told me to go back. Where are you?"

Lying in the hospital bed parallel to Jim's and afraid to believe her ears, Penny replied, "I'm here, Jim. I'm right beside you. Honey, are you all right? I'm sorry, that was dumb, I just want to know—"

"If I'm alive? I think so . . . ." Jim's whispery voice trailed away.

The ER doctor, quietly listening and watching, looked at Penny and said, "That was great. His vitals are coming back around, and his color is getting better. I think we're turning the corner. He'll go in and out like that for a while, but I think he'll make it, now."

"Oh God, doctor, I hope so. What next?"

"We didn't use much blood bringing him around to this point and I want to keep the transfusion going. And I want to have more blood ready if we need it, so I want to have you stay as you are. After we stop the transfusion, I'll get another unit of blood from you to keep in reserve. It should take less than an hour, if it's okay with you."

Tears in her eyes, Penny answered, "Yes, yes, yes . . . yes, it's okay with me. An hour, a day, whatever you need."

"Okay, just rest. The nurse will bring you something to help you handle your blood loss. I have to go out to talk to the sheriff's deputies waiting in the lobby."

Penny closed her eyes and sobbed uncontrollably, her upper body heaving and tears streaming down her face; her mind alternating between the terror of needing to shoot and kill a man, and happiness over Jim surviving his close brush with death.

"Who is that crying? Is that you crying, Penny?"

Penny choked back her sobs, squeezed the tears from her eyes as she rolled over on one side to get a full-length view of Jim in the adjacent bed, only a few feet away.

"It is me, Jim. I thought I was going to lose you. My God, I'm happy to hear your voice."

"What happened? I only . . . I remember that car coming up fast from behind and one of them . . . pointing a gun at me," Jim said in a halting, scratchy voice.

"You shot each other. I think you hit him first and then his gun fired and hit you and your motorcycle. The shot hit you in the leg and punctured the artery behind your knee. You nearly bled to death."

"I . . . I sort of remember two guns going off, but after that everything went blank."

"The gunshot damaged the top part of your engine and it froze. Your bike went into a skid and off the road, throwing you over the high side and into the ditch."

"What happened to the guys who were after us?"

"They're both dead, but we can talk about that later. We're going to have to go over it with the sheriff's men when the doctor okays it."

"I won't remember half of what you would tell me now, anyway. But I need to go over it before we talk to them. What are we both doing, side by side in hospital beds?"

"You've been getting a blood transfusion—from me."

Without a sound, Jim shook his head from side to side, trying to find something to say. At last he whispered, "Jesus, Penny, you're giving me your blood . . . to save my life. That's . . . that's the most wonderful thing I can imagine." After another silence, trying to find the right words, he continued, "I can't . . . I can't begin to tell you how it makes me feel that your blood is in . . . ." But he couldn't finish the sentence as tears rolled down his face from all four corners of his eyes, so he stopped trying, rolling his head from side to side.

Penny's eyes flooded at the sight of Jim's tears. The thought of strong, motorcycle riding Jim, crying his heart out made her love him more than she thought she could love a man again. The nurse who'd been patiently sitting and watching the two broke down in tears and excused herself, saying she needed to check in with the doctor.

After gathering her composure, Penny asked, "When you were first coming around a few minutes ago, you said something like, 'I'm coming, Penny. I'm coming back. He told me to go back.' What was that about? Who was telling you to go back? Do you remember that?"

Jim stared at Penny as though he were looking right through her, searching for an answer. "You're going to think I'm crazy, but you asked, so I'll tell you."

Jim hesitated, organizing his thoughts, "I believed I was dying, or even dead. You know those stories people tell of near-death experiences . . . and how they see an all-white space . . . with maybe a parent or some loved one, waiting for them there?"

"Yes, I've heard of those."

"Well . . . I think I was there, or in one of those. The white space was fading in the center, like—you know—receding in places like a fog will do when you're driving? As that happened I could see myself standing on a gravel road in farm country somewhere—it looked like the farm country back around my home in Indiana. A little way down that gravel road, there was a guy leaning across the seat of a motorcycle parked sideways across the road. He was smoking a cigarette and wearing a leather jacket with the collar turned up."

Jim stopped for a moment, as though doing a reality check on what he was about to say. He went on: "The guy was James Dean. He waved at me, like he was saying 'Hi'. I waved back and started walking toward him when he held up both hands, palms toward me like a 'stop' signal. So I slowed, but didn't stop. He pushed his hands towards me and was saying something I couldn't make out. Then I realized there was no sound—his lips were moving, but I couldn't hear anything. He kept doing it and I kept on trying to make out what he was trying to say. So I watched his lips to see if I could understand him that way. Then it was easy; he was saying 'Stop, go back to her,' and he pointed back behind me, like 'turn around'. And that's when I heard you saying, 'Jim, honey, can you hear me?'"

"Is that when you said, 'I'm coming, Penny?'"

"I guess so. Jesus, I was about to let myself step over the edge when I heard you calling me."

"I . . . I don't know what to say, Jim. I don't believe in the afterlife and all of that, but this is weird."

"Yeah, I know. I feel—used to feel—the same way," Jim answered.

"Yes . . . used to . . . . It's like someone—something—put James Dean in your dream."

"I'm not sure it was a dream, Penny."

The ER surgeon, who'd silently slipped through the curtains and listened to the conversation said, "Hi, you two. I'm a fairly agnostic person when it comes to things like this, but it's an amazing story and I know you're not making it up because I've heard it as you told it."

Both, still grappling with their mysterious experience, looked with surprise at the doctor and said, 'Hi' nearly in the same breath.

"But I have to suggest that this was all happening at about the same time the new blood would have been kicking in and bringing Jim back around. This could have been a hallucination that was a purely physical response—or it might have been something more than that," the doctor continued.

"Thanks doc, remind me to tell you about James Dean and me some time . . . ." Jim said.

"I don't want to try telling you what to believe, though. Could have been one or the other—or both.

"I like both: Penny's blood starting to kick in, and James Dean talking to me, telling me to listen to her."

"My money's on her," the doctor said before going on to tell them about what he needed to do to repair Jim's damaged popliteal artery and fix up his knee enough to get him back to San Diego. "An hour ago I didn't know if I would need to do any of that."

"Don't remind me, please. I wondered about it too. Can you make it good enough so I can be in our wedding up in Aztec on Wednesday? I don't want Penny to have to go alone . . . ."

Penny kicked the bed leg, "There won't be a wedding if you're not there, James!"

"Don't worry. You can make it in a wheelchair," the doctor added.

"Put a Harley Davidson decal on the seat back and I'll be fine, Doc."

"Good Lord, Jim, I think you are back," Penny said. "Did the police tell you I shot a man out there?" Penny asked, looking at the doctor.

"Yes, they did. And they told me there was a second man killed too. Sounds like you were in a war out there."

"God, it was awful, doctor. They came up from behind us with the car window down and a shotgun aimed out through it. It was us or them."

"I believe you, but what I believe doesn't make any difference. They'll want to talk to you about it when I tell them it's okay."

"I'm not looking forward to it. When do you think you'll okay it?" Penny asked.

"Couple of hours, maybe three or four. Jim needs to be completely lucid. You don't want him to make any mistakes."

"No kidding! Thank you. We can use the time."

"Look, take your time with your answers. And remember, you have the right to have an attorney present."

"Where would we get an attorney out here, in Shiprock? Are there any?"

"Mostly Indian Law attorneys; the kind that fight the government for Indian rights."

"I guess we'll try to answer their questions as best and honestly as we can. If it looks like they're trying to trap us, though, we may stop and demand an attorney," Jim said.

"Good luck. We'll stitch that artery up a little better now. And I'll have a technician from Orthopedics come in to fit you for a splint he'll make up and have for you in an hour or two. We'll let the police talk to you after that, if you're still getting better."

"Okay, thanks for all you help doctor. I don't need to tell you I wouldn't be here if it weren't for you."

"Thanks, but by the way, you have shotgun pellets scattered all around in your knee. We've removed the ones that were in your fatty tissue and muscle, but there are still more in the knee bones and cartilage. You'll need to go to an orthopedist in San Diego as soon as you can to get a plan to fix that. A total knee replacement may be the best solution."

"Uuuughhh," Jim replied. I hear the rehab for that is months."

"It is. Good thing you have this wonderful lady to help you through this!"

Penny smiled, and said, "I'm going to take good care of him; I want to make sure he can ride motorcycles again so we can finish this trip someday."

Twenty-Four - Vindication

The next morning, New Mexico's San Juan County Sheriff stood next to Jim's hospital bed. "Detective Morton in the SDPD confirms your story. He mentioned Mack Allen's arrest, the cabin raid, the murder in Ramona, and your trip here to New Mexico. But there are other probable associated crimes you may not know about. The owner of Needles Van and Truck Rentals was found dead, badly beaten, and floating in the Colorado ten miles downstream from Needles."

"Oh Jesus, they killed Fred over this, too?" Penny said in anguish.

"I'm sure they would have killed us, too, after they got whatever they were looking for. And even if they didn't . . . ." Jim added.

"Here are a few documents we need you to sign. They are admissions of killing the men in self-defense. There's one for you, Penny, and another for you, Jim. There's a statement in each saying that there will be no charges pressed against either of you now, or in the future, signed by our District Attorney."

"Do you mind if I call a friend who knows about these things, just to make sure we're fully absolved by these documents. We don't have an attorney, but this person is the next best thing."

"No, go ahead."

Jim called Paul Daggett and read him the documents.

"The wording sounds fine, Jim. I'd go ahead and sign them and get back here to California as fast as possible. California laws will protect you in case the wording isn't perfect. There isn't likely to be an extradition over wording. And, I don't think they're trying to set you up. Do you want me to talk to them?"

"It would make us feel a lot better."

There was a short, intense conversation between Daggett and the sheriff, ending with each giving the other best regards and wishes of good luck. Daggett then called Jim's cell phone and said, "Sign them, you'll be okay. But what about your leg?"

"I think it'll be fine when I can get back to San Diego and have an orthopedic specialist look at it and decide what to do."

"So, are you heading right back here, then?"

"No, we're still getting married by a shaman in a traditional cere-mony out here, first."

"When's the wedding?"

"Day after tomorrow. Want to come? You can fly out with Steve and Ali."

"I'd love to, but I'll pass and see you when you're back."

"Glad you've been around to help me out—again. See you back in San Diego."

As they were signing the documents, the chief detective asked them, each in turn, a final question. "Jim, were you sure there were no alternatives to shooting that man?"

"I'm going sixty miles an hour and a man I don't know is alongside me in a car, yelling something I can't understand because of wind and road noises, and he's making threatening motions at me with a shotgun. We've had indications of being tracked, our houses raided, and people we've dealt with in jail or dead. I had a split second to think about it and decided it was him or me. Hell yes—it was self-defense, and I'd do it again in a heartbeat."

"Okay, I believe you. You can add that statement at the bottom of the page if you want."

As Jim wrote the statement in a blank space at the bottom of the page, the detective said, "But you do understand I've got to write you up for carrying a concealed weapon without a permit. That carry permit you have from California isn't valid here in New Mexico. Do you want to plead guilty to that? The DA said she'd be considerate of what you've been through."

"I guess I don't have a choice. Yes."

"Okay, sign this plea."

Nervously Jim signed the guilty plea document. *What is this going to cost me?*

"In view of your clean record in California and on the recommendation of the SDPD, the DA is dropping the misdemeanor charge, and issuing you a warning to never carry a gun again in New Mexico without proper permits. But we are keeping your gun."

"I thought you would. I'll miss it, I've had a Colt .45 since I was in the Marines. But, what the hell, thanks, Sheriff. You've been great."

"Penny, what about you? Are you convinced there was no alternative to shooting that man?"

"He was a clear danger: a man who was threatening me, and then charged at me with a handgun. I had a fiancé gushing blood who would soon be dead if I didn't get him out of the way, and I had one or two seconds to think about it. As Jim says, hell yes—it was in self-defense, not to mention saving the life of my dying fiancé! I'd do it again in a heartbeat, too."

"Thanks, no further questions. You can add that statement on your sheet too if you want. You're both free to go."

"Thank you, Sheriff. The hospital wants to keep me around for another day, so I'll be here tomorrow, and then over in Aztec on Wednesday. We'll be out of New Mexico by Thursday if I can figure out what to do with our motorcycles."

"I forgot to tell you: I can help you with that. We had them both hauled to the Harley dealer in Farmington. They've been looking at ways to get the bikes shipped to San Diego. I'm sure you can work something out with them."

"You're telling me you knew how this was all going to end hours ago?" Jim asked.

"You never did look like the guilty parties from the minute I laid eyes on you. But, we had to do the investigation and the paperwork. Good luck to you both, and best wishes in your marriage."

Penny couldn't resist; she stepped over to the sheriff and hugged him, "Thank you, sir, thank you so much."

"Welcome ma'am."

As they sat on their side-by-side hospital beds, now in a real hospital room, eating the cafeteria's tuna casserole, Penny asked, "How are we going to get home? You can't ride with me on my motorcycle and I don't think you'd be comfortable in a rented car for a two-day drive. And I don't think you can get in an airplane seat with that leg sticking straight out."

"I know, I've been thinking about that. I'm going to call Steve to see if he can bring a plane that has the two rows of facing back seats arrangement. I think I can stretch out in one of those comfortably enough for three or four hours. But that's using the term *comfortable* very loosely . . . ."

"Good idea, we need to update them on everything, anyway."

Penny handed Jim his scratched and cracked cell phone with its still-working screen that looked like a jigsaw puzzle, "It's a little beat up, but it still works. I called myself with it yesterday to check it."

"What, no shotgun pellets in it?"

"Lucky thing it was in your pocket on the other side of your motorcycle."

Jim smiled, shaking his head at his wonderful fiancé and punched Steve's number.

"How's it going? Pretty wild, Steve. We were being chased by two creeps all the way over here to Farmington, New Mexico. They caught up with us on the way back from some ruins we were visiting and tried to ambush us."

"I guess you escaped, though?"

"Escaped? That's one word for it. More like we shot our way out of it."

"Shot your way out? Like with guns and bullets?"

"Yeah, guns and bullets. We won, and they lost."

"Doesn't sound like you wanted to negotiate with them. Are you both okay?"

"Negotiating is hard, side by side, at sixty miles an hour on a bad road. I'm a little damaged, which is why I called. My cycle is wrecked and because of a knee injury, I can't ride it back anyway—and I don't think I'll be able to handle a two-day car ride. I'm hoping you can bring a plane with the two rows of facing rear seats when you fly out here."

"Sure. What happened?"

"I got shot in the knee with a shotgun. Pellets in the bone and cartilage make it impossible for me to walk until I get a little orthopedic work done. It's in a splint so I can't move it—which would be too painful, anyway. They want it immobilized so I don't screw up the surgical work they did to an artery."

"Jesus, man; this sounds bad. Didn't I tell you we have a Bonanza A36 with that rear seating arrangement? It's the plane we were going to fly anyway!"

"Great! No, I didn't know that. So look, the plan stays the same then: we're getting married—with me in a wheelchair—at the same time and same place. But we can't meet you at the airport. If you rent a large SUV, like a Chevy Suburban or something, you can pick us up here at the hospital in Shiprock, and I can ride sidesaddle in the back for the short trips we'll make. I've already reserved a room for you two for Wednesday night, and Tuesday night, too, if you want to come tomorrow."

"I think we should come tomorrow. We'll be there Tuesday afternoon or early evening and call your cell when we've landed."

"Okay, that's the plan then."

"Jim, we didn't talk about Penny. Is she okay?"

"She's fine, Steve. I'm very proud of her, she saved my life—twice."

"I want to hear the story, but I want all four of us to be together when you tell it."

"You're right. And Penny should be the one telling it. She's a terrific lady."

"I thought so when we first met her. What about the bad guys, are they in jail?"

"No, they're in the morgue in Farmington. I shot one, and Penny shot the other."

"Holy Mother, I can't believe this."

"We can tell you the whole story Tuesday night, over dinner and drinks."

"Alice won't believe this. See you tomorrow."

Twenty-Five - Ceremony

The waitress in the quiet steakhouse had just left with their orders when Jim wheeled himself into the dining room to join the others at their table. He needed to update Steve, Ali, and Penny. "I talked to Morton while you all were having a drink in the lounge. He said they picked up the two guys who broke into Penny's place along with their boss; a guy named Carlos Garcia," Jim said.

"What's the story on them?" Steve asked.

"Middle guys in a drug ring operating in the Imperial Beach area. The big guys they work for are people SDPD know about and have been watching, but don't have anything on. Garcia had the notebook in his car when they busted him. It was under the passenger seat along with some other stuff: maps with notes, a cell phone full of photos of street people and street corners with street signs and buildings. It looks like he was trying to verify the information in the notebook by finding the dealers working their territories. He had drug paraphernalia on his person, so they were able to search the car."

"What do the police think they were up to with the information?" Penny asked.

"Who knows; start a territorial drug war? Move in on territories by taking out the dealers? Or squeeze the dealers and force them into their network or gang? All the above—and more?"

"I wonder if the two we ran into out here and those three are all the people we need to worry about. Or are there others involved who know about us?" Penny asked, fidgeting and biting a fingernail.

"Morton said they needed to move on the top guys in Carlos's gang to determine that. But, this operation had to be too important for the top guys not to know. They want to shut them all down as fast as possible and warn them to lay off us," Jim answered.

"Glad to hear that," Penny said, looking a little more relaxed.

"But do they have anything on them?" Steve asked.

"That's the sixty-four-dollar question. My impression is that they don't."

"There had to be cell phone conversations flying all around given the stuff that Penny and Jim stepped into," Ali said. They must be able to trace who was calling who and discover the other people involved."

"They're working that: trying to trace calls from the area between Needles and Farmington back to San Diego. If they can find who the dead guys' phones called back in San Diego, they've got something to work with. Same with the two guys who broke into Penny's place: find the numbers they were in contact with during the days before and after the break-in. They can't get the conversations, but they can find out who was contacting who," Jim said.

"I think that'll take a while," Ali replied, frowning.

Penny asked, "What's 'a while?'"

"Probably weeks," Ali said. "They've got to get the cell phone companies to cooperate, which means a court order—and assuming that happens, they can get copies of the call logs. Then they'll have to run searches through the logs looking for the callers' numbers and who they called. After that, they need to look at the frequency of calls to each call recipient to get an idea of who was being called the most. And after that, they need to get names of the persons with the highest number of received calls. It's a lot of searching and analysis work."

"But they must have software tools to help with that," Jim said.

"Sure, but it depends on how up-to-date they are, and how well-trained, too." Ali replied.

"How do you know all this, Ali?" Penny asked.

Ali lifted her drink, as if in a salute, "Too many years of doing the same thing—not on phone calls, but on hackers' electronic signatures."

"All we can do is hope for the best," Steve volunteered. "In the meanwhile, we've got a wedding tomorrow. Let's drink a toast!"

The dim entrance tunnel, slanting down to the dirt
floor of the Great Kiva in Aztec, New Mexico

"Why isn't he wearing buckskins and feathers? He looks stupid in that cowboy hat," Jim complained.

"Shhhh. He's telling us what we're supposed to do," Penny whispered.

"The groom and bride will enter from this east entrance, walk clockwise around to the west side and wait for the others. The family members and friends will follow and be seated on the floor behind the bride and groom. Please enter now," the shaman-justice of the peace in low-heeled boots and a tall, Hopalong Cassidy-style hat with a deep dent high on the crown front ordered in a solemn voice.

Jim and Penny followed the orders, Penny pushing Jim in his wheelchair through the narrow, tunnel like entrance. She rotated the chair around to face the shaman as he finished explaining the ceremony, which first consisted of Penny taking water from a gourd and washing Jim's hands, followed by Jim doing the same for Penny. The shaman then drew a cross from east to west and north to south with yellow corn pollen dust on the surface of a basket full of blue corn mush. He instructed the two to eat generous finger-pinches of the mush from each end of the pollen cross; Jim first, followed by Penny. They were to start with the east end of the cross and eat their way, clockwise, around the four compass points. Jim hesitated, not sure he'd understood the instructions: *what the . . . .*

"Jim, you're supposed to go first!" Penny whispered, edging the wheelchair forward and nudging him with an elbow as they began the ceremony, centered in the Great Kiva under the glare of ceiling-mounted flood lamps.

"Do I have to? That blue mush doesn't look like something I should eat," he whispered back. "I don't ever remember eating anything that was blue."

"You have to. This is what you wanted, a traditional ceremony."

"I was thinking more of peyote and mezcal. Why don't you go first?"

"The shaman said the man goes first, followed by the woman. It's symbolic for her committing to follow him forever after."

"Are you going to do that?"

"Shhhh, don't talk so loud . . . . Maybe . . . Depends . . . ."

"On what?"

"I don't know. You keep finding good bike rides for the rest of our lives?" Pointing, Penny said, "Take a pinch of mush from that side of the bowl, for God's sake! Then after I do the same, work your way around going clockwise. I'll move your chair if you can't reach it."

"Okay, but I don't think I'm going to like it."

"Shhhh!"

"What were you expecting, dear, an evening with Carlos Castañeda?" Penny asked.

"Ha, yes, with chants and dancing around the fire, ghostly images of warriors silhouetted on the kiva walls, and peyote and mezcal?" Steve laughed.

"No, not Castañeda, but a little more mysticism than eating mush out of a wicker basket from all four points of the compass under those mega-watt bulbs on the ceiling. And he could have worn some traditional clothes, you know, like buckskins and moccasins, with some feathers somewhere. Jeans, boots, and a cowboy hat just didn't do it for me." Jim's face showed a touch of mild, but happy sarcasm.

"But look, hon, it was traditional and pleasant, and a long way from 'dearly beloved'," Penny said. "The atmosphere in the kiva, with just the faux fire in the center lighting the ceremonial meal was nice. He couldn't help it that the rules don't allow real fires in a national monument. And he did have ceremonial paint on his face, and he did speak part of the ceremony in traditional language. I liked it!" Penny said.

Ali added, "I liked it too, and he had his chest covered with strings of beads."

"So did I," Steve joined in. "And he did have a feather in his hat!"

"So there; three of us liked it and I'll never forget it, honey. Please don't be negative."

Jim snickered an ironical, "Yeah, a single scrawny feather curling out of his hat band, like Bob Dylan's in 'The Last Waltz.'" But he then brightened. "Yes, you're all right; I'm just bummed out over this knee and my motorcycle. But the hell with that, I'm still alive and I've just married the woman of my dreams. Besides, we got two for one: the face paint gave us a shaman and the cowboy hat gave us the justice of the peace. We needed both, one for originality and the other to make our marriage legal everywhere. I need another drink!"

"It has to be my last one since I'm the pilot tomorrow, but let's have one more toast. Another round of mezcal, bartender."

"Looks even more barren and lonely from up here at ten thousand feet than riding a motorcycle through it," Penny said to Jim as she looked out the rear window at the slowly passing desert landscape.

"Yeah, it looks better when the sun is low in the morning or early evening with all the shadows and softer colors. And the viewing angle from ground level gives you a completely different perspective. Looking straight down on it from this altitude in mid-day sunlight, everything washes out."

"But this is the way to get back to San Diego fast if you need to," Penny replied.

Jim groaned as he painfully shifted his leg to the other rear facing seat, and said, "I know. But I'd rather be down there—in it—than up here if I had my choice. It's too sterile this way. I want to feel the heat—or cold—smell the surroundings, feel the highway, and see things up close."

"Are you complaining about Barton Airways back there?" Steve asked. Everyone had their headphones plugged into the cabin COMM system.

"Hell no, man. This is the best way to travel with a fucked-up, in-a-splint leg ever invented. No offense meant, Steve, I'm still irritated over having to abort the trip because of those bastards," Jim said, trying to sound nonchalant in spite of the danger and deaths.

"Steve was just having a little fun with you," Ali said. "Have you thought about how you'll get around to see doctors and go to clinics to get that leg fixed?"

"Not in my Porsche, for sure. We can push the front passenger seat all the way back in Penny's Mustang, recline it to the max, and I'll wedge myself in like I'm riding in an airliner, back in the cheap seats. My Scripps doctors and clinics are easy to get to and within fifteen minutes of my house. Don't worry, Penny will take great care of me and get me where I need to go."

"I know she will, Jim."

Steve slipped back into the conversation. "Hey, Jim, you should check in with Morton at SDPD early tomorrow to find out what's going on."

"Yeah, we will. By the way, did I mention to you that they kept my gun back there at Farmington? That piece will cost me six hundred dollars to replace!"

"But you're not sitting in a jail cell."

"Yeah, I can't complain. And it saved our lives, so I guess it was worth it. But, you know what? Wouldn't it have been ironic to have been locked up, just like Wyatt and Billy?

"And have an alcoholic lawyer in the next cell? If you ask me, there were too many similarities between your trip and 'Easy Rider'. I'm thinking of the shot-gunning out on that Louisiana highway." Steve said.

"Jesus, you can say that again," Penny said with a bitter frown.

"Never thought that movie could almost become our reality . . . like an omen. I'm starting to get spooked over the stuff that's been happening lately, like the James Dean dream, and now this." Jim said.

"And some strange calendar coincidences we've had, too," Penny added.

Ali, confused by the conversation, asked, "What are you talking about back there? Sounds like you're weirding out," as Steve backed off the throttle to begin the descent to San Diego's Montgomery Airport.

Penny and Jim looked at each other, wondering how to answer the question. Penny finally said, "It's too hard to talk over all the background noise in the plane. We'll tell you about it sometime . . . ."

Twenty-Six -
Starvation Mountain

Jim's La Jolla Colony house, several weeks after returning from New Mexico

"You're right dear, that king-size bed of yours looks a lot better in here than that old lumpy twin of mine. But I'm not sure about those flowery drapes."

"Get used to them, James. I'm not living with those burlap-looking things you had hanging in here. And I know you're going to like my big bed . . . ."

"I'm not asking why you had it . . . ." dodging the pillow she threw at him.

"Admit it, don't you think you needed some new things around the house to get rid of that stale, man-cave atmosphere you had?"

"Yes, I have to admit it. This place needed your touch. Now we've got the best of both of our things."

"We have to talk about that medieval desk and credenza soon . . . ."

"No, not negotiable. Those have been with me since I lived in Los Gatos."

"Reminds me too much of that horrible old desk Mack had up at Ramona. I want to forget about him and that whole ugly story."

"Okay, I can understand that, hon. But you need to give me some time to find a replacement that feels right."

"What do you think is going to feel right?"

"I don't know, maybe something oriental . . . . Ali might have some good ideas."

"I think you're right about that. She did a great job with their cabin in Julian and has good taste in clothes. She's a very stylish lady."

"But so are you."

"Okay, we can have a fun day; the four of us tripping through stores in La Jolla and around San Diego, finding your new office furniture."

"Tripping is the right word, with this crutch and stiff leg! Not sure that I'll be able to afford you, now that we're married."

He dodged another pillow. "Too late Jim Schmidt!" Jim went down the hall to his office to answer the ringing phone.

"Hi Jim. Can you get Penny on the line, too, if she's there?" Dale Morton asked Jim.

"Sure."

"Penny, it's Detective Morton. He wants to talk to both of us," Jim yelled into the hallway.

Penny hurried into Jim's office where she'd been setting up her new computer to view the cameras they'd brought from her condominium and installed around Jim's La Jolla Colony house, now her home, too.

"Hi, Detective Morton," she said.

"Hi, Penny. I've got either good news or bad news, depending on how you want to look at it."

"What is it?"

"Mack Allen is dead. We found him in an alley in the Gaslamp district last night. He'd was shot—in the face."

"Oh my God!" Penny exclaimed. "I . . . I don't know how to feel about it. He was a good guy at one point, and then all this happened. I never thought he meant to harm me. I just got caught up in his stupid so-called 'businesses.'"

"Well, intentionally or not, he almost killed you both. I don't imagine you'll be sending flowers."

"No, no flowers . . . ."

"Any clues about who did it?" Jim asked.

"No, there were no witnesses and we haven't found any evidence yet. We'll be checking security cameras in the surrounding businesses, but it looks like it happened in the alley where there's no lighting. This will probably be a case where we have to roll someone who'll want to bargain for reduced criminal charges—who we haven't even caught yet. The drug world can be a black box when it wants to though."

"It has to be related to the notebook and what he learned in putting it together, don't you think?" Penny asked.

"Probably. It's likely someone in Garcia's gang; someone getting revenge and keeping him off the streets so he's no longer a threat to the networks."

"What about us? Do you think this eliminates the danger for us?" Jim asked.

"We can never say for sure, but it might. Now that the notebook maps are out there, and Mack was the one responsible for exposing the networks—and he's dead, there's no sensible reason anyone should have a motive to go after either of you."

"Sensible! These people aren't sensible!" Penny exclaimed.

"But crooks do have a logic they work from. They don't want to take unnecessary risks and give the police more reason to be looking at them. If they don't feel they have to do something in the interests of their businesses, they won't. They don't murder people just for the fun of it, or to get even—unless they're trying to send a message to someone. And we think they must know by now that you were both caught up in Mack's games by accident. They should be smart enough to know those two you shot in New Mexico—supposedly pros—are dead because of their own stupidity. So, the bottom line is that we'll be ending the plainclothes stakeouts we've been doing at your place over the last two months."

"We're not happy to hear that, but I guess we understand. How are you doing rounding up those names in the maps? Are you doing any major damage to the networks?" Jim asked.

"So-so. We've been picking up a few street dealers and trying to roll them for information, but have had only a few successes, so it's slow work. They've changed most of the street people and moved them around, so it's getting hard to work it at that level. We're trying to move on up the chain and get the distributors and money people. It's hard, slow work, unless we get lucky and have a major break."

"Yeah, I expected that," Jim replied.

"But it has slowed down the trafficking. We're getting a lot fewer ODs and 911 drug emergencies, so that's a good thing."

"Can't expect miracles, I guess, but those are worthwhile results." Jim said.

"No, we don't expect miracles. But this has been one of the biggest breaks we've ever had, so no one downtown is complaining."

"Great! By the way, now that you're ending the stakeouts, I'll want to carry a gun. Will I still have my permit?"

"Sure, we don't have any reason to revoke it. But you do have to update it to show what you're going to carry."

"Same thing, Colt .45."

"That was fast."

"Had two, both legal."

"You're an interesting guy, Jim."

"How so?"

"You keep surprising us."

"Me too, detective," Penny added with a smile.

"How's that leg doing? Are you back on it and riding motorcycles?"

"My leg is too stiff to bend enough yet, so I'm still hobbling around with a crutch. They took out everything they could get to, but there's still some buckshot scattered around in there that I'll have to live with. Since the shifter is on the left side, and I don't have good leg movement control yet, I can't shift. I'm getting there, but I'm still a few weeks away from it."

"Must be hard on you, not being able to ride. I know you love it."

"I'm riding . . . ."

"How? Did you fit on a hand shifter?"

"No, those are suicide. I'm riding behind Penny!"

"Now that's got to be a good ride."

"Yeah, and I get to squeeze her the whole time."

"Okay, I don't think we need to go any further with—" Morton said.

"No, you *don't* need to go any further," Penny said, cutting them off, but laughing.

"Goodbye you two. Stay in touch," Morton said, ending the call.

"He's a good guy, Penny."

"Yes, he is. I didn't expect so much co-operation and keeping us up-to-date as he's done."

"Let's call Steve and Ali to see if they want guests for the weekend."

"Oh, good! I'd love that, Jim."

"But, why don't you plan on staying longer? Like a couple of weeks to let things cool down in San Diego. If the police are going to stop giving you protection, maybe you both should disappear for a while. Stay up here with us; Alice loves having Penny around to talk with."

"Well—"

Steve cut him off. "What else do you have to do? You're retired—for good this time, right? And Penny's between jobs—if she's going back to work—and I doubt she's in a hurry to do that after the Ramona mess."

"I know, I know. Penny doesn't have to go back to work at all. We don't need her to bring in any income since I have everything paid off: house, car, motorcycles, and money in investments. I told you I had my finances set for retirement; it works for just me or both of us. But she'll do whatever she wants after we get settled in."

"Yeah, she seems very independent."

"You know, I think staying with you for a little while is a great idea." He held the phone out so Steve could hear his conversation with Penny who had moved to his back and circled her arms around his waist. "What do you think about spending two or three weeks in Julian with Steve and Ali?"

She squeezed him, saying, "In a heartbeat! Let's go before they change their minds. But I want to finish setting up the video recorder for remote viewing and recording on my new PC. I want to have that working before we leave; never know what you'll find creeping around your house."

"Not a bad idea, dear," Steve said.

After two weeks of easy trail walking in the nearby mountains, allowing Jim's leg to get stronger and gain more flexibility, the foursome wanted down time for rest, reading, and conversation. Ali was still demanding to hear about the James Dean events Jim mentioned on the plane trip returning from New Mexico, and the strange synchronicities Penny had hinted at. Jim left it to Penny to tell everything, preferring to hear her version and interpretations rather than his own. He found it interesting and touching that Penny told of the James Dean incidents, including Jim's hopes for a mystic connection, with no derision. It was a story too many would tell with a subtle put-down, rolling eyes, manner. He loved her sincerity.

Penny stopped at various points in the story, offering to let Jim pick it up from there or add points she'd missed. He declined each time, knowing there was little he could add. He wanted it to be her story, too.

Penny also described their coincidental meeting on Starvation Mountain on the fifth anniversary of Annie's death. An occasional tear slipped from her eye as she spoke of the motorcycle accident that killed Bruce, but avoiding her marital problems. She also touched on Annie and her part of Jim's earlier life, so together with her loss of Bruce, Steve and Ali could understand the context of their relationship.

After nearly two hours of this, Jim could see exhaustion in Penny's face and that Steve and Ali's eyes were glazing over. "Let's go over to that winery and see what's on the menu."

"Thought you'd never mention it," Steve answered.

Julian Mountain Winery, near Ali and Steve's place

"And I thought I knew you, Jim. You keep surprising me," Ali said, pouring everyone a glass of Pinot Noir.

"Me too," Steve added. I worked with you for years and never heard any of this."

"Just never came up. And I don't make a habit of running around telling everyone about my love life."

"Can we do this again, occasionally, for the next few months? I feel like we're just getting to know ourselves," Ali asked, holding the Pinot Noir bottle up to the waiter, nodding.

"I'd love it, but are you sure you won't get tired of us being around too much?" Penny responded.

"God no. You two are a breath of fresh air. I love living here with Steve, but we need stimulation from the outside now and then. Our house is big enough, and you two are so easy to have as guests that I'd like to do it more. Please say yes."

"What about you, Steve, are you up for it?" Jim asked.

"I want what Alice wants. The answer is; of course. Besides, I have some new crypto projects you might be interested in. So, it's agreed then. You'll come up and stay for a week or two, every few weeks—until we're tired of it."

"Who gets to make that call?" Steve asked.

"Anyone. Anyone can and no one will question it. We'll just know it's time, then."

Ali and Steve's Julian cabin, six months later. The friendship still strong after multiple visits by Penny and Jim.

Penny and Jim had loaded their small suitcases in Jim's Porsche, Steve standing near the driver's side door. Penny was slipping her aviator style sunglasses over her ears, being careful to avoid snagging her hair when Jim said, "We have to break this routine for a while, Steve. I need to spend more time at the new house on the mountain over the next couple of months. The studs are all up and I want to see that the Ethernet cabling is being installed the way I want it, and that the access point and server closet is being built and wired correctly. If they don't do it right and I don't find the mistakes until after the walls are finished, I'll hate myself for not being on top of things."

"Yeah, I understand that. This place was built in the '80s with no thoughts of home broadband and computers. I had a hell of a time getting it the way I wanted; took me months," Steve said.

Ali walked out to join the three as Steve and Jim were finishing the conversation. "Jim just told me he needs to spend a lot of time up at the new house, double checking things that need to be right before they seal up the walls. I can't argue with it. I'd do the same."

"Does that mean our fun times together are ending?" Ali asked, a faux pout on her face.

"No, not at all." Penny answered. "It's just an interruption. After it's done, you two will be our house guests in the same way."

"I'd love it!" Ali answered. "But can't we see it sooner? Do we have to wait until it's finished?"

"No, you can come up to see it any time. How about this? I'll wait until there's enough completed that you can see what it's going to be like when it's done, and I'll call you and we'll meet there."

"Why don't we bring food and wine and have a picnic on the slab?" Ali proposed.

"Great idea. But we don't have to sit on the slab, there's a cool rock-pile at the edge of the property overlooking the entire San Pasqual Valley. We can set up our picnic on a big, flat rock that's there, and look at the view and sip wine!"

"Done. Looking forward to your call," Steve said.

Two months later. A late afternoon picnic on the large flat rock at the edge of Jim and Penny's construction site with a half-completed house in the background.

"My God, look at that view. This is beautiful. How did you find this place?" Ali asked.

"Just out riding my motorcycle one day and saw the 'For Sale' sign. Bought it the next week," Jim said.

"Why is it called Starvation Mountain? Look at all the avocado and citrus trees everywhere; how ironic!"

"There actually is a historical reason. General Kearny and American soldiers fighting in the Mexican-American War were surrounded around here in 1846 with no supplies. They had to eat their mules."

"Okay, don't tell me anymore. I hate hearing how the animals suffered in wars back then," Ali said, frowning.

They sat around the big, flat rock, eating finger food and sipping wine from crystal glasses Ali had brought. They watched the hawks and buzzards soaring on mountainside thermals, and then coasting out high over the valley floor, watching for prey on the ground. Jim pointed out the surrounding mountains, naming them, and giving their peak heights until everyone's eyes glazed over and they had to signal for a time out.

"What, no interest in the world around you?"

"You told us all this when we hiked Volcan Mountain months ago, remember?" Penny laughed.

"Wanted to make sure you remember. Steve needs to know those peaks, so he doesn't fly into one."

"They're all shown on my charts, Jim. And I always fly by my charts and NAV systems—which also have the peak heights."

"Okay then, but no one here gets a merit badge for geography."

"You could use a little more wine, Jim. Let me refill your wine glass. So, Penny, that little cabin we saw when we drove up here is the place you were staying in when you met Jim?" Ali asked.

"That's the place. It's the place that was raided when Jim and I were up in the Central Valley looking for James Dean's ghost—or spirit—or karma, whatever . . . ."

Suddenly Jim's facial expression changed to a look of being overtaken by a new thought. "Penny, do you think that Harley is still back there, behind the cabin?"

"God knows. I don't care, either."

"Well. I was just thinking; Mack went to jail while you were up here at the cabin and stayed in there for several more weeks, and then was murdered not long after being released. I doubt he made it up here to get it.

And his partner, Gary, was murdered right after you moved to my place, so I doubt that he came to get it in the day or two he had left. I bet it's still there."

"Why do you care?"

"It's a damn nice Harley. If it's there, I want to see if I can arrange to buy it in an estate auction at a good price."

"I don't want that, or anything of Mack's around. And you don't need another motorcycle, dear. But, go check it out if you must," Penny said, shrugging her shoulders and smiling at him. "I'll never ride the damn thing!"

"Might make a great conversation piece, or it could be used as a trade-in for a newer bike. I'll make a quick run over there, it won't take me ten minutes. Be right back."

He sprang up with no trace of the knee injury from the gunshot wound and trotted up his new driveway and crossed over to the gravel driveway leading to the cabin. He was in sight most of the way until he cut over to the gravel driveway. The three continued talking, Penny saying, "He can't stop talking about the mountains he's been on around here—"

A bright flash of light with the blood red flames of a large explosion, followed by a thunderous bang, came from the direction of the cabin. A huge cloud of dust and smoke rose into the air as small pieces of debris fell and settled on their picnic cloth.

"Jim!" Penny shrieked. "Jim! Jesus Christ that was right where the cabin is." She jumped up and ran toward the cabin, dodging through the trees rather than taking the longer way up the driveway and back down the cabin's gravel driveway. Steve and Ali followed her, fifty feet behind, unable to catch up because of the rough terrain between the trees.

They caught up to Penny standing at the end of the gravel drive, shocked and staring at the horror of the destroyed cabin. The back had been obliterated and the front and side walls leaned awkwardly in toward each other. The rear wall of the cabin was scattered around the lot in pieces, like a jigsaw puzzle carelessly thrown away.

"Where is he? Oh my God—everything's destroyed. The motorcycle should have been on the far side—behind the cabin—but there's nothing there." She pointed at the place where the little three-sided lean-to once housed the Harley. Even the cabin's concrete foundation fractured in places from the force of the explosion, and large sections of cinder block lay on the ground.

Steve ran to the place Penny had pointed to, but there was nothing more than splintered boards, fractured cinder blocks, roof shingles, and fragments of cabin materials.

"Oh Jesus; where is he?" She broke down in tears, hunched over, with both arms clasped across her stomach. Ali ran to her and wrapped her in a tight embrace, trying to console her.

"Oh God, I don't want to lose him, Ali, I love him so much."

Trying to console her and give a reason for hope, Ali answered, "Maybe we'll find him farther out from the cabin. Maybe he wasn't that close and just got knocked down and is in the trees somewhere, unconscious."

Choking back tears, Penny said, "Let's look around the edges of the clearing."

The three walked in circles on opposite sides of the clearing, hoping to find Jim, uninjured, lying against a tree, but fearing they'd find only body parts. Steve called 911 as he headed toward the area of the lean-to where the Harley would have been stored.

As Steve neared the spot of the missing lean-to, he saw a hand extending out from under an intact, eight by eight piece of sheet metal. "Here! Here he is," Steve shouted. "He's under this big piece of sheet metal."

Penny and Ali ran toward the place where Steve was struggling to lift the big piece of corrugated sheet metal. Fear and hope tore at Penny's mind: *What would they find under that piece of metal? Had it protected him,*

*or did it maim and tear into him with its sharp edges? Would he be alive, or
. . . she couldn't think of it.*

They helped Steve carefully lift and slide the metal off Jim's body.
"He's breathing but looks unconscious!" Steve loudly said, unable to
restrain his emotions.

"Oh God, look at those cuts on his face and arms," Penny moaned.
"Call 911 again, please, Steve. Tell them we've found him."

Steve called 911 to give them the update and ask about their progress
in reaching the site. He verified they knew how to get to the cabin. Penny
knelt beside Jim, trying to get a response, "Jim, honey, can you hear me?
Are you awake? Please say something if you can."

There was no response throughout the long minutes it took the 911
team to reach them, load him into the ambulance, and the drive to nearby
Palomar Hospital. Penny rode in the back—again.

"He's breathing okay—slow—but okay, and his cardio measurements
aren't too bad, ma'am."

"How bad are the cuts? Is he going to bleed to death?"

"I don't think so. None of the cuts hit any arteries or major veins. We
should be able to handle the worst of the cuts on the way to the hospital
and take care of the rest once we're there."

"But why is he unconscious?"

"This."

The medic rolled Jim's head sideways to point out a place where he'd
suffered a powerful blow to the head. There was only slight external bleeding, but the swelling had already produced a golf ball sized lump that was
pushing out through his long thick hair.

"Oh, Jesus. That looks terrible." Penny whispered.

"The driver has already told the ER we're going to need neuro people
when we get there."

Four a.m., twelve hours after the explosion

The neurosurgeon sat down beside Penny. "We've inserted drainage tubes into his head to get the fluid off his brain. It's not blood, and there's no internal bleeding inside his head, but there is fluid collecting on his brain that is causing pressure, which has to be relieved."

"What now, doctor?" Penny asked.

"Wait. We wait until the fluid has drained out, and the pressure comes down—and hope he recovers consciousness. Then we have to see that there's no recurrence of fluid buildup again before we can say he's out of the woods."

"What if the fluid continues to collect there?" Penny asked.

"Let's hope that doesn't happen. If it does, it'll require major surgery to find where it's coming from and what's causing it. From there, it's hard to say. Major cranial trauma cases are unpredictable."

"Jim, honey, can you hear me? Are you awake?"

Hunched over in her chair at Jim's bedside, arms wrapped around her stomach, crying intermittently for hours, Penny had been waiting for any sign that Jim was coming out of the near coma the doctors had put him in. She'd repeated the hopeful questions to the unresponsive Jim so many times she was losing hope. Penny couldn't believe where she was again, so soon after the experience in New Mexico. It seemed like a nightmare—but it was real—too real. *God, what will I do if I lose him?*

"Penny, is that you? Are you crying? I'm coming, dear, I'm coming." Jim muttered through cracked lips, as though talking in his sleep, eyes still closed. His eyes flickered open for a second before closing again. The eye opening and closing process repeated again and again before his eyes finally snapped wide open. A lost, confused look came over Jim's face as his eyes scanned around the room until they focused on Penny, sitting up in astonishment and hope.

She slipped out of her chair for the single step it took to get to his side and leaned over to kiss him on the forehead, taking care to avoid all the tubes.

"What happened? I was running toward a cabin and that's the last I remember."

"We were on Starvation Mountain at the new house and you wanted to see if that motorcycle was still behind the cabin. Something exploded when you were there, and . . . now you're here. And I'm here, and Steve and Ali are here—we're all here, praying for you."

Penny turned to the nurse who'd been standing off to the side and asked, "Can our friends in the waiting room come in for a minute?"

"I'll check with the doctor, and if he says yes, I'll go out to escort them in so you don't have to leave."

A few minutes later, Steve and Ali tip-toed cautiously into Jim's little curtained area in the ER, staying back from the bed. "Hi Jim, you sure have a thing for emergency rooms," Steve quipped, trying to lighten everyone's mood.

Ali went around to the far side of the bed where she leaned over and planted a soft kiss on Jim's cheek, saying, "We're so glad to hear you're coming out of it."

"Hi Ali, Hi Steve. S . . . sorry to put you through this," Jim whispered.

"Look who's here," Steve announced, as he ushered Detective Dale Morton into the crowded area.

"You must be tired of me by now," Jim croaked, coughing and trying to laugh.

"Never. You four make my otherwise boring life interesting. I just wanted to come by to see you and to let you know we have a team up there with the county sheriff's crime scene people. We want to see if it has anything to do with the drug project we've been working on in the city. I'll get back to you as soon as we have anything definitive."

Morton shook everyone's hand and left as the doctor pushed the curtains aside and stepped to Jim's side, looking at the myriad of digital displays. The nurse insisted that everyone but Penny leave to let a tiring Jim rest.

"We're going to discharge you tomorrow if all the vitals continue to look good." The neurosurgeon told Jim and Penny.

"Great! A full week in a hospital is too long. I've had more fun in here than I can stand," Jim said with a big smile.

"Well . . . it could have been a month or longer if that piece of sheet metal hadn't shielded you from taking the full force of that blast. Or, it could have been just a five-minute visit . . . ."

"I hear you, doc." Jim said, looking at Penny, who was shuddering at the thought.

"I'll see you in the morning for a final checkup and sign out. By the way, there's a detective Morton waiting to see you," he said as he turned to leave.

"Hey, Dale, what's new?" Jim said as Dale Morton walked up to the bedside.

"Here's what we've got, but it's not much. The bomb was in the motorcycle's gas tank. It peeled it open like a banana. The explosion tore the bike into three pieces that scattered in different directions. The front wheel and handle bars were in the trees on one side of the clearing, the engine was still in the same place by the cabin, covered by debris from the cabin wall, and the rear wheel assembly was blown in the opposite direction into the trees just outside the clearing. It was a damn powerful bomb."

"What set it off? Any ideas or evidence?"

"No evidence. Our best guess is that it was either a pressure sensor or motion detector hidden on the cycle—probably in the seat. There weren't any of the signs of wireless devices or timers that the bomb squad usually find when those are the trigger mechanisms. You didn't touch it, did you? If you were close enough to touch or sit on it, you wouldn't be here."

"No. I remember that as I was coming up to the back of the cabin where the bike would be, I stumbled a little and fell against that corrugated sheet metal wall that formed one side of the lean-to. It was only a second after that when I think the explosion happened."

"There were shelves on the inside of that wall. You may have knocked something off a shelf that hit the bike and set off the bomb," Morton said.

"I guess that stumble saved my life. The sheet metal shielded me from the worst of the blast."

"Nothing like being clumsy at the right time," Morton tried to joke.

"So, it was a booby trap waiting for someone to sit on it?"

"Probably."

"Who? Mack? Do you think it was intended to kill Mack and had been set up before he was shot downtown?" Penny asked.

"Possibly," Morton replied.

"But why wouldn't they have come out and disarmed it so no innocent person would get killed?" She asked, but knew the answer as she asked the question. Penny and Jim glanced at each other in horror, both now realizing the truth.

Morton stood silently for a long while, letting it sink into Penny and Jim before saying, "Mack probably wasn't the target, at least not any longer."

"Jesus Christ! The murderers; the bastards. Why?" Jim said bitterly.

"It could be Mack was the primary target, and after he was killed, Penny became the secondary target—or both of you became the targets. It would have killed you both."

"But why? We weren't trying to do anything to them," Penny said through clenched teeth.

Morton shrugged his shoulders, "There's no explaining crazy people. We're going to get them for you, I promise."

"Jim, I told you I'd hate myself if my stupid decisions ever got you hurt. And now this happens—right next to your dream home. I'm so, so sorry—"

Jim cut her off, saying, "Penny, it's 'our' dream home. If it wasn't for what you call a stupid decision, we'd never even have met. I'll take a little danger to not having you at all. We'll deal with it, hon."

She leaned over the bed, no longer needing to dodge an array of tubes, and kissed him lovingly on the mouth. "You keep finding ever more wonderful things to say. I love you, Jim Schmidt."

Riding back to their La Jolla Colony home from the hospital in Penny's Mustang, Jim repeated the question Penny had just asked: "Why was I saying, 'I'm coming, dear. I'm coming,' when I was first waking up in the ER?"

It was just like when you were coming out of it in the ER in New Mexico, almost the same words."

"You may find this hard to believe, but I was in that white space again, on the same gravel road in farm country somewhere, and the same motorcycle was parked crossways on the road, just like in the last dream—if it was a dream. But this time, the bike was there—with no rider. James Dean wasn't with it."

"He wasn't there to tell you to go back this time?"

"No, there was only a leather jacket hanging on the throttle side of the handle bars—and a pair of aviator sunglasses on the seat."

"Oh my God, Jim. This is getting too strange. It's like this dream has become your guardian angel."

"But that may be over, now."

"Why do you say that?"

"I didn't stumble over my own feet or trip on something on the ground when I fell against that wall of sheet metal. I lost my balance . . . because I saw him there . . . as I was approaching the cabin."

"At the cabin?"

"Yes, it was the same thing: a white space, the gravel road with a motorcycle parked sideways across it, and Dean standing beside it. He was giving me that palms-up, pushing sign again, and mouthing 'Stop'. I was so surprised, I lost my balance and fell against that wall."

"Jesus! He was there to save you again?"

"I guess. And the fact that the last time I saw the motorcycle—without him—when I was coming around in the hospital, you know . . . just the leather jacket and sunglasses on the bike, makes me think it was a message."

"What? What do you think was the message?"

"You're not going to see me again; don't count on me anymore."

"A last message . . . from a rebel—without a cause . . . ?" Penny's voice softened and faded.

"Seems like it. But I think he did have a cause."

"A cause? What do you think it was?"

"It was about you. It was always about you."

"Me? What about me?"

"Making sure I'd hold onto you and we'd stay together."

The End

Robert Gilberg

Acknowledgments

Anne Marie Welsch: my critic, book doctor, consultant, and friend.

Leslie Wolf Branscomb: my copy editor and proof reader.

Alice Chang, for gracing this book with her, and a few of her friends' presence in this book.

The spirits of James Dean, Wyatt, and Billie.

Van Morrison, for the use of a few of his lines.